Through the Ashes

Jack Lawrence

Through the Ashes

Other Titles by Jack Lawrence

David Thorne Series
Blood Thorn
Bed of Thorns
Thorn Lake

Standalone Titles
I've Been Waiting

Dedication

To all the readers. Without you, none of this
would be possible.

Chapter 1

His rifle's sights were trained directly on his target's heart. The tip of his finger gingerly rested on the smooth trigger. When he was ready, he would squeeze the trigger, causing his target to be dropped before his eyes even reopened after the blast instinctively forced a blink. He had killed before. A part of him, some part deep inside, still felt a little guilty about the act. It was always a messy endeavor, and he wasn't sure how to feel about the power it provided. His prey would be living, another day unfolding just as any other. Less than a fraction of a second later, they would be dead. Without warning, just gone. But he had also noticed that the more he did it, the easier it became. The less those thoughts crossed his mind. It became just part of his life. He rationalized it was something he had to do. It was a necessity for his survival now. Ethan Barret took one last breath, steadied his sights, and squeezed.

The explosion from his rifle rang out into the otherwise empty world; the smoke hung in the crisp October air as the cold seemed to trap it in place. Rifle season in Indiana didn't technically start for another week, but it was his land. Who was to tell him what he could do on his land?

When the smoke finally dissipated, he saw the results of his actions. The six-point buck, its life extinguished in a matter of moments. It was only the second deer he had ever shot, but he had killed other animals to fill his freezer. He would have never thought he would find himself there in his past life. Sitting in a makeshift blind, built of dead limbs and fallen trees, hunting animals to feed himself. But that was his life now. Part of it was freeing. Part of it was jarring. He couldn't help but think how his daughter, Mary, would've felt seeing him there now. She had such a loving heart. Even his wife, Kristina, would have had a thought or two. She would have laughed at him in second-hand camo, his toned face caked with mud because an old-timer he met in town when he moved in said deer could see the flesh of a man's face. She would have scolded him for taking the animal's life when he could make the hour's drive to town.

But he lived a different life now. He was a different man. A lot had changed over the past year. He was no longer the Senior Prosecuting Attorney of Indiana. He no longer lived off six figures or spent time with influential people. In fact, he hadn't shaved in three months, for the first time knowing what his face looked like with his thick brown beard growing in. He hadn't cut his hair either, so it had become tousled more often than not. Most days, he didn't recognize the reflection he saw in his mirror. He didn't think his family would have either; if they had seen him, he would have been as much a stranger to them as he had become to himself.

He took a moment to watch the woods. The leaves had finally turned two weeks before. Now, the brilliance of the reds, yellows, and oranges sparkled in front of the setting sun. He felt a calmness come over him. Ethan hadn't counted on how much peace being alone in the woods on a fall evening could bring him. When his mind usually ran with no end in sight, moments like these brought him to a place of stillness. The pallet of colors danced rhythmically above him, and they couldn't have cared less about the world around them. He only hoped he could find a time where he could say the same about himself.

Ethan pulled the bolt back, then pushed it forward to seat a new round in case the animal was not dead. He wanted to make sure it wouldn't suffer.

Ethan left his blind, confident the animal had bled out, though he couldn't know for sure. The sun would set in twenty minutes, but it would take him at least twice that long to dress the animal. Then, he would have to drag it two miles to his truck before making the ten-minute drive back home.

He had made a mess of the first deer he tried to dress and didn't want to do that again. This meat, he hoped, would last him at least a year. The other one would have, had he done better at dressing and butchering it. The small game and the vegetables he tried to grow would not last him until the spring, let alone the following fall.

As he dropped to his knees, he retrieved the old knife he bought at a pawn shop from its sheath. He wondered if he would even make it a year. He wondered if he would make it another week. The loneliness was growing to be nearly unbearable at times. The guilt suffocating.

His thoughts drifted back to Mary and Kristina. They would have liked the cabin. It wasn't fancy — only one bedroom and one bath with leaking fixtures—but it sat on ten acres. The previous owner had carved a walking trail throughout the property, which they would have loved. There was a bare spot on top of the hill behind the cabin where Kristina would have planted a garden, and Mary would have wanted him to build a swing. They finally could've bought that dog Mary had been begging for over the past three years—since her fourth birthday. Kristina would have loved it if he had finally been able to pull himself from work.

He thought about calling Beaver, his old irritable neighbor he met when he first bought the cabin the previous fall. The man promised that after their last hunt together, he would be happy to help in any way he could. Having someone to help carry the 170-pound carcass would be nice. Except that would mean having to talk to someone. That carried more risks than he cared to deal with. Besides, Ethan reconsidered; he had become much stronger over the past year, his hands more calloused and overall more capable. It was something he needed to do himself, without burdening anyone else.

Chapter 2

Ethan showered the dirt and blood away after he had processed the meat in his shed. He had filled the freezer, which brought a moment of pride, but like most good things, it faded quickly. He was left there alone. He went to the fridge and retrieved a cold Miller, popping the top and taking a solid gulp from the can.

Despite his better judgment, he grabbed his phone from the counter on his way to the living room. The fire burning in the wood stove lit the way to the couch. He sat down and turned on his television, scanning his living room to keep his mind busy. If his mind were busy, he wouldn't think. The square room was fifteen feet by fifteen feet, housing only a small television with five channels and a DVD player, a small coffee table he had found on the side of the road, and the raggedy couch he found himself sleeping on most nights.

When the bare room no longer interested him, he turned to his phone. The twenty missed calls, and forty unread texts only brought more anxiety. Undoubtedly people reaching out to remind him it had been a year. Suddenly he felt absolutely alone. He had been ignoring the sounds of his phone for a few days, but that didn't stop the sender's attempts. Ethan groaned as he tossed the phone to his side, digging in his pocket for the bottle of pills.

He pulled it free, opened it, and poured the contents onto the coffee table. Vicodin had been prescribed to him three years before, after oral surgery, to remove an infected tooth. He didn't know how many it would take or even if they were too old to work. But he didn't want to use the rifle. He didn't want whoever would find him to have that image stuck in their mind.

He just wanted the thoughts to stop—the memories—and especially the guilt. Ethan knew how different his life would be if Kristina and Mary were there with him. He had tried even though he wasn't as good of a husband or father as he had always wanted to be.

Ethan picked up the pills, feeling them roll in his palm. His phone beeped twice, but he ignored it. He looked at the picture of him, Kristina, and Mary at the ski lodge two years before. Mary sat in his lap smiling, not knowing sadness then. Her hazel-colored hair was hidden by the cap, and her matching eyes were protected by a thick pair of goggles. Kristina looked tired, but her eyes and wide smile showed she believed there was still hope that their marriage would work. Ethan looked happy, but he knew he was probably thinking about some case. One he couldn't recall now if he wanted. Yet, that case and many others had taken away from his family. He had never even attended one of Mary's soccer games. Now, he knew he never could. He pulled Kristina's gold chain from the frame's right corner. The cold metal in his hand returned him to when he had given it to her. It had been their first anniversary, when he took her to her favorite restaurant, Maggiano. She had worn a blue dress that flattered the natural curves of her body, highlighting the bits of green speckled around her iris. He slid the chain into his pocket, returning his attention to the pills.

His phone began ringing, but he tuned it out as he always did. Almost as soon as the ringing stopped, it started again. He dropped the pills back on the table and switched the phone off, tossing it with his complete frustration.

Ethan grabbed the pills again, ready to silence everything around him. But an eager knock at his door broke his mind from the darkness. The knocking intensified with each thudding boom.

Chapter 3

Ethan felt an uncomfortableness settle over him as he approached the door. Not many people knew where he was, and Beaver only came around if Ethan had done something to piss him off, which he hadn't done in months. He had refused the state's offer to protect him, and he felt he could do just as well on his own as they could—but really, he wanted to have some control over the situation. Now, he wondered if he hadn't made a mistake. Ethan eyed the rifle leaning against the wall near the door. He knew there was still one 30-06 round in the chamber from his hunt earlier in the evening. But with a bolt-action, he only had one shot.

The knocking continued as he pulled the chain and flipped the latch. He pulled the solid maple door open, his shoulder on the edge to help push it shut if needed.

John Waters seemed relieved to see the door move. Ethan was surprised to see John standing there but not too surprised. John was one of the three people who knew he was at the cabin, his childhood friend who had been the balance in his life before he met Kristina.

John's six-foot-two height seemed dwarfed as he leaned against the frame of the door. His dark hair and deep brown eyes looked almost black against the night behind him. He wore the same stupid IU sweater he had worn since college, which had gone from a deep red to a sickly pink over the years. Holes rendered it useless against solid winds, Ethan always said.

"What are you doing here?" Ethan finally asked once John's silent stare and look of disapproval had become too uncomfortable. Their eyes were even with John leaning against the frame.

"Not going to invite your best friend in to get warm?"

Ethan shifted his body to allow the door to open a little more, just enough for John to squeeze in. "You didn't answer my question."

"Well, Bud, it's been almost a year, and you haven't answered anyone's calls or texts in days. Your mom asked me to check on you to see if you were holding up okay." John's eyes shifted over to the table with the white rectangle pills still sprawled across is. "Not a moment too soon, I see."

Ethan shifted his weight as he closed the door. "I just had a headache."

"Well, that'd take care of it," John smirked as he talked. He had never been comfortable with tense situations, a self-proclaimed lover, not a fighter. He made his way to the couch, plopped himself down, and began pushing the pills into a pile before replacing them in the bottle.

"Can I get you a drink?" Ethan asked, heading toward the kitchen across from the living room before John could speak. "I got water and beer."

"Water. I like the new look, by the way. A beard suits you."

Ethan ignored the comment as he retrieved two water bottles and returned to the living room. He took the vacant spot next to John. "Where are you staying tonight?"

"Here," John responded flatly.

"Then you get the couch," Ethan forced a yawn. He had minimal human contact in the past year: a few conversations with John, a weekly call to his mother, a weekly check-in with the police back home, and a dozen or so interactions with Beaver. He had grown used to the isolation. The pills were in his peripheral, and he realized if he had become used to it, it wouldn't have made him grab the pills in the first place.

"So not much different than at home."

"You and Margo fighting again?" Ethan inquired. John and Margo married the year after Ethan and Kristina. She was a flamboyant French woman who thought she should've made it as a model, except that she met John, who held her back. Of course, her crooked nose and too-wide eyes had nothing to do with it in her mind. Every couple of years, when she started to long for more, she would blame John for not letting her reach her potential, then cast him off to the couch while giving him the silent treatment for a week or two. Ethan doubted she knew about John's infidelities, or she would've left him years ago.

"Well," John started, rotating his head in discomfort, "she went to stay with a friend about six months ago. She said she needed time away. I got the divorce papers last week. So, this little trip is a bit of a vacation for me. Get some guy time in."

"It has been a long time," Ethan admitted. "What time are you heading home tomorrow? We could grab lunch or something before you head out."

A menacing smile spread across John's face as he slapped Ethan's back as if hammering the point home. "I'm not leaving until I'm sure you aren't going to get any more *headaches*."

Ethan swallowed hard, burying the frustration. "Don't you have a job?"

John's smirk returned. "They won't miss me."

"Lawyers don't take vacations," Ethan pointed out.

"Which is why I have so much time built up."

"Well, winter will be here before too long. If you're here, don't think you get to lounge around; I'm putting you to work."

"What exactly constitutes *work* around here?"

Ethan leaned back onto the couch, his own smirk emerging. "You missed the hunting phase. But now we must gather enough firewood to get through the winter, pick some apples, harvest some fish, and ensure everything is insulated before the freeze comes."

"It's Indiana, Ethan. You have at least until January before you have to worry about that."

Ethan shook his head dismissively. "It comes quicker out here."

"You spend a year in a cabin, and suddenly you're Mr. Pioneer."

Ethan shrugged. "It's good for keeping the mind at bay."

John nodded as if he understood. John had been there when Kristina and Mary were killed. He was there when the police couldn't track down Angel Vargas after he threatened Ethan in open court and Ethan's home was burned down two days later, with his wife and daughter inside. John was there when Ethan had his meltdown, leaving everything and everyone to move into the cabin. At first, people understood it was for safety since Vargas hadn't been apprehended. It was also customary to have a breakdown after losing one's entire family. But now, it seemed to be too much. As if a year passing by would be enough time for him to move on.

That first winter taught Ethan a lot about self-reliance. Had it not been for Beaver, he would have never shot his first deer that fall. He would have had to go into town, which was something he hoped to avoid as much as possible. The cartel Vargas ran with reached beyond just the cities bleeding into the small towns. Ethan feared being recognized and word getting back to Vargas about his whereabouts. Beaver was the one who told him how much wood it would take to survive a winter when the only source of heat was a rusted wood-burning stove.

"When will you be coming home?" John asked, breaking Ethan's roaming thoughts.

Ethan hadn't noticed how much he put behind him when he came to the cabin. Seeing John brought it all back. Perhaps, he thought, that was why he rarely answered his phone.

"I don't know that I will," he told John honestly. "I enjoy it here. It's calmer. Plus, what would I do? Certainly not practice law."

"Why not? You were the best-damned prosecutor the state ever saw. You could go to just about any firm, and they'd hire you on the spot."

"That's not home for me anymore, John." Ethan stretched his back against the rear of the couch, desperate to move the tension rising there. "This is. Without Kristina and Mary, there's no reason to go back," Ethan then added, "And Vargas still has a bounty on my head."

"How long can you honestly survive here? You're pushing forty. Stuff starts falling apart after that."

For the first time in recent memory, Ethan felt a smile. "I feel younger than I have in decades. All the work keeps me young. Plus, if I get decrepit, there's a Wal-Mart an hour away. In ten years, there'll probably be one at the end of the road."

"What about money? Even if you live as a caveman, you need money."

Ethan ran his hand through his beard. Kristina would have hated it. "Between selling the lot from the house last year, my retirement fund, and all the money we stocked away since we got married, I suspect I could go on forever. I bought the cabin and land in cash. Taxes and utilities are low. I don't buy anything. So far, not even my food. My only high expense is the cellphone."

John gave Ethan his cocky smile. The one he gave when he managed to talk Ethan to follow his way. Ethan had noticed it since they first met in law school, something he had grown to dislike more and more over the years.

"What?" Ethan asked.

"Nothing. Just got you thinking about the future, which means you won't need these anymore." John stuffed the orange bottle he had refilled into his jeans pocket. John stretched his arms high and let out a vicious yawn. "Got any pillows and blankets in this shack? I'm exhausted."

Ethan suddenly remembered John could irk him more than anyone. But he was still glad to hear a human voice and he was thankful John knocked when he did. What John didn't realize was that Ethan thought about the future a lot. It just never helped.

Chapter 4

Ethan was awake at 5 a.m. He shoved a new log into the stove and blew on it gently until the dying coals ignited the fresh wood. He put his kettle on top, the same as every morning. Except this morning, his normally peaceful ritual was interrupted by John's grinding snore as he lay sprawled across the couch with a quarter of his body handing off the edge.

Once steam escaped the spout, he poured it into two mugs. Then he dropped a scoop of instant coffee into each one, stirred them, and put one on the table in front of John. Ethan gently nudged John's leg with his foot. The deep gargle of John's snoring sputtered like a choking car, before he shot up.

"What's happening? Everything okay?" John's questions came out rapidly, his eyes not even open as he tried to process what had interrupted his sleep.

"It's five-fifteen. Time to check the trail cameras." Ethan leaned back on his heels, relishing the torment.

"I thought you didn't buy anything. Where the hell did you get trail cameras?" John rubbed the sleep from his eyes. Out of instinct, it seemed, he reached for the coffee to fuel his consciousness.

"They belong to a neighbor. But he lets me check them since our property lines butt up. That way, I know where to go if I need to hunt."

"Didn't you say you just shot a deer?" John looked up to Ethan with one eye squinting open. "Which is super barbaric, by the way."

"I did. But I can always use some small game and prepare for next season. There are also coyotes and bobcats out here that kill everything else. So, I like to monitor it."

"And this is a job that requires two grown men?"

"No, but I told you, if you're going to be here, I'm putting you to work."

"Fine," John growled out. "What else is on your ridiculous agenda for the day?"

Ethan smirked and took a long sip from his coffee to take a little more pleasure in seeing John fidget. "That's a surprise."

Ethan adjusted the rifle sling around his shoulder as they made their way through the woods. They had gone two hundred yards. Ethan had reminded John twice to keep his voice low when he spoke. John remained silent the rest of the walk to the first camera. He watched in amazement as Ethan unstrapped the device from the tree, flipped it open to retrieve the SIM card, and then replaced it just as he had found it.

In the past year, it became another part of Ethan's day. Something he just did. Growing up in the city with a doctor and housewife, going to college in the city, then living just on the outskirts of the city himself as an adult, he could count on one hand how many times he had been in the woods. But with survival on the line, a person learns quickly, or they die. Despite his moment the previous night, Ethan knew he didn't want to die. If he did, he would've attempted to track down Vargas on his own in the past year.

"What do we do now?" John asked, following Ethan to the next camera.

"We'll check the last two, have lunch, cut some wood, then check the cards. I like to make notes of what's on there so I can learn their patterns. Then we can do whatever we want."

"And you do this every day?"

"Depends on the day. Some days, I have to focus on stocking up food. Some days, I mostly focus on repairs or improving the property. On other days, I focus on wood. No two days are the same."

John failed to lift his foot high enough to clear a log as they passed it. He stumbled, fortunately catching himself on a nearby tree.

"How are those feet treating you?"

"Hush," John scolded. "I'm a civilized human. I don't spend my time in the woods like a caveman."

"You'd never survive out of the city, John. Not enough women to keep you satisfied anywhere else."

"You know me so well," John agreed. Then, he stopped, pointing ahead of them. "Who's that?"

Ethan's eyes followed his finger. Two hundred yards away stood a man in brown overalls covering a thick coat. An orange hat sat lazily on his head. Ethan gave a gentle whistle, causing the man to turn in their direction. He gave them a nod before he walked away.

"Crotchety old bastard," Ethan mused to himself.

"You know him?"

"My neighbor," Ethan replied with a nod. "Beaver."

John's face contorted into a look of confusion. "What the hell kind of name is *Beaver*?"

"Well, I doubt it's his real name," Ethan admitted. "He has a big beard and the teeth to match. It's suiting."

"You gave up five-star restaurants, a six-figure salary, and rubbing elbows with the most powerful people money can buy to live in a run-down shack next to a man named *Beaver*."

Ethan recognized it sounded like a jab to John, but to him, it sounded even better than paradise. He had never known there could be such complete quiet in the world until he moved to the cabin. He couldn't remember the last time he had seen the stars at night—if he ever had—before moving here. Everything out here moved faster, but in the ways that mattered, so much slower. He smiled before starting to walk again.

Chapter 5

Ethan and John descended the hill behind the cabin. When Ethan put his arm out in front of John, like a firm gate, John stopped. "Man, I'm freezing," John blew into his hands before rubbing them with determined vigor. "Why are we stopping?"

Ethan pointed to something near the bottom of the hill, but John couldn't tell what. He followed Ethan down the embankment until he stopped. Ethan kneeled in a muddy patch twenty yards from the back of the cabin. He looked to John's foot, then back at the mud. John took a single step to his right so he could see what Ethan was staring at.

"Did you come back here last night?"

"No," John confirmed. He finally saw the footprint that had caught Ethan's attention. "It could've been from when we left this morning."

Ethan shook his head. "We went around the right of the house. We didn't come this way."

"Maybe it was your neighbor, Beater."

"Beaver," he corrected, knowing John was deliberately being insolent. "He would've come to the front of the house if he needed something. Besides, these are too small to be his."

"You know the man's shoe size? How close are you guys?"

Ethan stood, taking a deep breath of the fall air to gather his thoughts. "He gave me a pair of boots last winter because I didn't have any. They were too big. These prints here are a little smaller than mine."

"Guess you do have poachers after all."

Ethan bit down hard on his teeth. His heart began to thump as anger grew in his stomach, he clenched his fists to direct the anger expanding within him. "It takes a real worthless scum to come out here and poach someone else's property."

John took a step back from Ethan, afraid he may become caught in the explosion if Ethan blew. "Relax man, who knows how old those tracks are. What if they weren't poachers at all? For all you know, it was someone from the water or electric company."

Ethan shook his head. "They've already been out this month to read the meters. And the tracks weren't here yesterday when I went hunting."

"Well, I'm cold as hell. I'm actually looking forward to chopping some wood. Might finally be able to get warm."

Ethan couldn't help but chuckle. "Well, John Waters ready to do work? It must be cold because hell has finally frozen over."

"You make jokes," John said wrapping an arm around Ethan's shoulder. "But I can work hard when there's something in it for me."

"Ah, yes. That checks out."

Ethan began walking again, pointing to a pile of tree stumps on the other side of the property.

Dozens of three-foot-long logs, two feet in diameter, rested next to a larger log sat upright. "Luckily for you, John, we have plenty of wood to chop."

"I already regret sounding so excited."

"It'll be fun," Ethan jested. "You'll get your first blister."

"I got blisters when I was sixteen, thank you. I played guitar for a year. That's how I got all the girls to give me their number in college."

"Speaking of which," Ethan opened his unlocked door and entered the cabin. The stove had kept the interior a warm seventy degrees, which hit his face as soon as he entered. He leaned his rifle against the wall. "Now that Margo's gone, have you found the replacement?"

"You know I'm never going to settle down again. Life's too short."

"People change," Ethan pointed out. He looked around the cabin before adding, "Obviously."

John nodded. "Not everyone gets the chance to change."

Chapter 6

By 3 p.m. Ethan Barret and John Waters had chopped enough wood that the pile rose to their waists. Ethan brought his wheel barrel out from the crawlspace under the front of the cabin, wheeling the wood to the overhang of the front porch each time John loaded it. When they finished, John was drenched in sweat, despite the temperatures being in the low 60's. John shifted and stretched his body in multiple directions hoping to release some of the tension and soreness but finding no luck.

"If you're sore now, wait until tomorrow."

"Who in their right mind would choose to live like this?"

"Me. For one," Ethan retrieved the axe from the base and tossed it into the wheel barrel. "Ready for lunch?"

"Yes! What are we having?"

"I have a rabbit in the fridge."

John's lip turned upward in revolt. "I'll eat none of that."

Ethan smiled. "I didn't think so. I have some bread and bacon."

"The essentials."

After they finished their lunch, Ethan went to his room to get his laptop. There was a time in his life he spent the better part of sixteen hours a day on the damn thing. Now, he spent less than an hour a week on it. Cracking it open only when he needed to check the SIM cards. He charged it twice a month, only once more than he would charge his cell phone.

He inserted the first card and began skimming. John was interested at first, marveled by the foxes, deer, and squirrels frolicking in front of the lens, clueless to the fact they were being spied on. Twenty pictures in, John lost interest. He went to the couch to flip through the five channels provided by Ethan's satellite, knowing there would be nothing to catch his attention.

Systematically Ethan continued through the SIM cards. He marked the times animals came in, which direction they came from, and which direction they went to. He came to the last card, feeling fatigue begin to set in. There had been more activity than normal and a process that usually took him only ten minutes had dragged out to nearly half an hour. He could hear John snoring from the couch. With any luck, John would get tired of Ethan's new way of life and excuse himself by tomorrow, leaving Ethan alone. Just the way he wanted it to be. Then he wondered if that was a lie he told himself.

He inserted the final SIM and began the process of scanning the photos. The third to last stopped him. That familiar feeling of anger returned, and his flesh turned cold despite the cabin's temperature resting in the mid-70s.

"John," he called out, spinning in his chair to face the couch. "John!"

John's eyes burst open as he turned his startled attention to Ethan. "Please tell me there isn't more work to do."

Ignoring the comment, Ethan waived him over. "Come check this out."

John walked over, leaning over Ethan's shoulder to get a clearer look at the screen. "What am I looking at?" To him, all he saw was a black blob crossing the right part of the frame.

"It's a person."

John squinted, trying to see what Ethan saw, but couldn't find it. "How the hell can you tell that?"

Ethan took his finger and traced the outline, pointing out the shoulder, the neck, and the back of the person's head. The way the sun had been oriented put the figure into a shadow. It would have been better had the person crossed it at night so the infrared would have been on.

"How do you know it isn't your neighbor?"

"Because when he passes the camera, he makes it a point to stop in front of it and wave, so I know it's him. I do the same."

"When was this?"

Ethan checked the time stamp. "About ten minutes before we checked it."

"I didn't see anyone else out there besides him."

Ethan's anger gave way to something else. Something he hadn't felt since his wife and daughter had been murdered: fear and helplessness.

Ethan turned to face John. "Someone followed you out here. You lead them right to me! They could have tracked your phone."

John took a step back, his hands raised in peace. "No one followed me. Why would they? I've never been here before and it's been a year. No one would have any reason to think I was coming out to see you last night."

"Then why is someone on my property just twelve hours after you show up?"

John shook his head, unable to find any answers. "I would not intentionally lead someone to you, Ethan. I know how to tell if I'm being trailed. I didn't see anything. Besides, you have a phone too. What's to stop them from tracking your phone, or anyone you've called in the past year?"

Ethan took a deep breath, pushing the emotions trying to surface back to where they belonged. He didn't have the energy to explain to John that he had created a system that made tracking him by phone more challenging. Not to mention, out here, service was spotty on the best days. His signal would not be reliable. Instead, he opted for a truce.

"Okay, I'm sorry. I may have overreacted. Maybe it is all a coincidence. But we need to keep our eyes open. If someone did follow you, we both know they aren't just wanting to have a chat."

"Good thing you have a gun and a paranoid neighbor," John offered, but his body began to hunch as he spoke. Ethan knew that meant he was getting anxious. Then he said, "What about calling the cops? If nothing else, someone is trespassing."

Ethan shook his head. "The cops won't be able to do anything with a boot and a quarter of a picture. Plus, I don't need them to know about my history."

"Why? Seems like someone in your situation would want the police to know all about it."

"They aren't equipped to deal with the cartel. They can't help solve my family's murder. There is nothing they can do except get in the way."

"Well, I can't leave now. Shame too, I was thinking about how nice my jacuzzi would be tomorrow." John put his hand on Ethan's shoulder, showing he was there.

Chapter 7

Just after the sun set, Ethan put on an extra layer of clothes before grabbing the extra trail cameras he had in his room. One of them the previous owner had left, and three more Beaver had given to him when he decided to upgrade to the ones out there now.

"Where are you going?" John inquired, his feet propped up on the coffee table, rolling a frozen jar of broth along the top of his leg.

"Going to put these around the property. If someone is out there, I want to know about it."

John's eyes narrowed in uncertainty. "I'm not an expert in this sort of thing, but if you can only check the thing after you've got the memory card out, won't they be long gone before you even know they've been there? Not to mention the fact that going into the woods at night kind of makes you an easy target."

"Same as with any other animal. I can plan accordingly if I know where they're coming from and where they're going. And I know these woods a lot better than they do. I'd hold my own out there."

John let out a cackled laugh. "You're a former prosecutor who has spent exactly eleven and a half months in the woods. You're not a Navy Seal."

Ethan pulled back the bolt of his rifle to ensure a round was seated in the chamber. Satisfied it was, he pushed the bolt forward, hanging the rifle from his shoulder. "No, but they've never been in these woods. It's thick and uneven. They'll make noise if they're trying to walk through it."

John's head swayed left to right. "It seems a little paranoid. For all we know, someone was just out on a hike and didn't realize it was private property. Or your neighbor forgot to waive just this one time. We both know these kinds of guys don't fuck around. If they'd found you, we'd be dead already."

"I don't put anything past Vargas. Are you coming, or are you just going to be a pain in my ass?"

"Can I do both?"

"So far, that's been the M.O."

"Then why break president?" John forced his body up from the couch, grimacing at the pain in muscles he had only just rediscovered a use for. Ethan smirked, remembering how sore he had been the first few months at the cabin.

"It's supposed to snow tonight. Not much," Ethan said as he opened the door, heading out into the darkness. "But it should be enough to see any prints if someone does pass through."

"Where are you going to put them?"

Ethan scanned his property, placing trees from memory as the night began to swallow the world around him. As the sun lowered behind the trees, leaving only a gentle hue of light in the distance where there were no trees, most of the property became cloaked in darkness. He had four cameras. One he would aim at the house, one at John's car, and one behind the house. The last one, he debated, should either go on the road leading to his cabin or in the ravine to the west, because that would be the best way to sneak onto the property with limited detection.

"Okay," Ethan finally said, handing two cameras to John. "Just strap these to the trees, flip the tabs on the side, and hit 'ON.' Latch it back up and you're done. Put one on that tree facing your car," he instructed, pointing toward a thick Musclewood tree ten yards from where John had parked. "Try to conceal it where that one branch comes off low, but not so the lens is obstructed. Put the other one over there." He pointed to his right where a line of Yellowwood trees stood. "Put it a little higher where the leaves have fallen. That'll help conceal it."

"Where are you going?" John asked hesitantly.

"Down to the ravine and back toward the hill behind the cabin. When you're done, just go back into the cabin. Toss another log in the stove."

"I would love to," John said. "Thing is, I don't have a weapon."

Ethan shrugged. "Like you said, if they wanted us dead, we would be. This is just precaution."

Ethan started at the back of the house, knowing it would be the easiest spot to access in the dark. He ambled, using the damp earth to his benefit to keep quiet as he stepped. The moment of peace, of absolute quiet, was refreshing. After so long being on his own, John's presence was twofold. It was nice having human contact, introducing his oldest friend to his new way of life, and having someone around who knew the pains he dragged around like an anchor.

But it was also exhausting. Far more tiring than the physical labor of living his new life. The energy it took to carry a conversation, to recall the past, to think of things outside of his everyday life had drained him. His mind felt heavy, and a headache had creeped somewhere in the back of his skull from the day. Now he had the concern of someone trespassing on his property to add to it.

He began to think John had been right, perhaps it was paranoia. Even if it were someone just passing through, that posed a risk to him. He had sacrificed everything he cherished for a career he thought he loved. If someone had found him it could have posed a threat to his life. It could also pose a threat to his mind. He didn't want to have to relive everything he had spent the past year trying to forget.

He tried to forget the argument he and Kristina had on the phone as he was leaving the office. An argument they had hundreds of times it felt like, about how he was never home. About how many of Mary's events he had missed. About how things needed to change. He didn't want to remember Mary crying because he had promised to take her trick-or-treating but had gotten stuck at the office and missed it. He didn't want to think about his wife telling him she was getting tired, knowing that when she said it, she meant she was getting tired of him. Tired of feeling like a single mother. She was tired of feeling stuck.

That night he decided he would change. He could resign his position and take on a smaller caseload with a private firm. He could teach, he could do almost anything else to show his family they took priority. As he drove home, he could see the thick black smog billowing over the other houses in his neighborhood, but it didn't register to him that it had been in the direction of his house. He pulled over as the emergency vehicles barreled past him, hoping for the best for whatever family had just lost their home. It wasn't until he parked a block from his house—what was supposed to be his home—and saw the violent blaze that the realization started to set in. The police had blocked the street, and even then, he hadn't *fully* processed that it was his house he watched burn.

It wasn't until Mrs. Flanning, their neighbor, rushed to his car, squalling in terror, that it all became undeniably real. At that moment, he scanned the crowd, looking for Kristina and Mary, yelling for them from inside his car. She had been the one to open the door, his screams, and her cries blending, forcing the other on-looking neighbors to turn their eyes from the blaze to them.

Ethan stopped. He forced the memories back where they belonged. Deep in his mind where he couldn't think of them, somewhere they couldn't come back to haunt him.

Alone in the woods, John was entirely out of sight, so he gripped the stock of his rifle. Instead of pulling it around, he screamed.

Chapter 8

"You tryin' to wake the dead, young man?" The raspy voice behind him was seemingly carried by the darkness. But Ethan recognized the graveled voice, which always reminded him of his grandfather who had taken a bullet to the throat over in Nam. Except Beaver lacked the scarring.

Ethan turned to face the man. Beaver was a force on his worst day. He was glad he had never found himself crossing him on a good one. Ethan had to tilt his eyes up slightly to meet Beaver's, who bragged about his ability to sneak up on his game, even at six-three. Ethan had seen him lift a two-hundred-thirty-pound deer over his shoulder as inconsequentially as a bag of laundry. Of course, Beaver likely outweighed the deer by fifty pounds. Beaver's long white beard danced on his shirt from the music of the breeze. The beard was stained by years of nicotine and stale coffee.

Ethan knew the man standing across from him had no idea how much Ethan wished he could accomplish such a task. "I've had someone sneaking onto my property. I guess I let my anger get the best of me."

Beaver nodded, acknowledging his anger had gotten him into his fair share of trouble also. "I was wonderin' about that. Saw a car going down the drive late last night. Then thought I saw a man out over by the ridge who looked like he had no business bein' there. Never could catch up with him, though."

"Did he run?"

Beaver nodded, spitting off to the side for the sake of it. "I ain't think he saw me. When I got to the ridge, he was gone, though."

"Think it was the same guy?" Ethan scanned the darkness around them, knowing someone could be ten yards from them and they would never know it.

"Couldn't tell ya. Keep them cameras where you put 'em, I'll put some up too. We'll catch the sonofabitch."

"What kind of car was it?" Ethan asked. If Beaver had spotted John trying to find his cabin, he wouldn't have wanted to work himself up over it. If it was someone else, that could be a problem.

Beaver's eyes flared as his mind tried to work. Ethan assumed if it wasn't a Ford or Chevy pickup, the man didn't know or care what it was.

"Some black city-folk car. Didn't catch the plates or nothin'."

John's car wasn't black, but it was dark. "Did you see it at night?"

Beaver's head bobbed, spitting again.

"Well, I appreciate you checking on me. I'll keep you posted about what pops up on the camera."

Beaver pointed with his head, "You got a better gun?" he asked, pointing to the rifle slung around Ethan's back.

"I think this one is just fine."

"Naw. It's good for deer and droppin' a man from far. But if someone's on your property or in your house, you want somethin' small. Somethin' you can shoot quick like. You miss with that, you waistin' all your time just tryin' to get the next shot in the damn chamber."

Beaver hunched over, reaching his long arms down to his ankle. He rolled up the bottom of his brown overalls, retrieving a small revolver. He handed it to Ethan. "That's a .38 six-shooter. No safety or nothin'. Just pull the trigger, and boom, she goes. But like I said, you only get six. I seen your aim with a scope, so don't go thinkin' you're John Wayne."

Ethan smiled as he took the gun. He knew it would be going directly into the drawer. Even if he found the trespasser, he had no intention of shooting them. He realized John was right. If Vargas had found him, he would likely already be dead. If Vargas were casing the cabin, his team would hit it so fast, that he wouldn't have the time or the firepower to stop them. In a best-case scenario, it was a single trespasser whom he felt he could catch and scare off.

Worst case, he hoped to be able to know how many, get John out of there, and take as many of them out as he could.

"I appreciate it," he told Beaver as the mammoth man returned to the woods.

Once he was alone again, Ethan scanned the area close to the house. There was no way John hadn't heard him scream. Nervousness began to fill his chest, his heart hit a rhythm that nearly buckled his knees. He put the pistol in his front pocket, then pulled the rifle up, the barrel pointed toward the ground in front of him.

He went to the front of the cabin, moving the barrel from right to left as he scanned the area. When he reached the front of the cabin, he heard John's uncertain voice. "Thank God, you're alive!"

"What the hell are you doing in there?" John had taken up hiding under the front porch, tucked behind the woodpile and the house's foundation. Under the upper deck's shadow, he was hidden in complete obscurity. Even as he stood, Ethan could only make out the silhouette.

"I heard you scream. I started running toward the back of the cabin and saw you standing next to that giant guy."

Ethan rolled his eyes. "You're a coward. You were going to leave me to be eaten by my neighbor? A lot of help you are."

"I could've ID'd him once the police got him." John tried to maneuver around the log pile but found himself caught.

"Future reference," Ethan began, "I wouldn't hide there. That's where the Black Widow's hunker down."

John's eyes went wide which only made Ethan laugh harder as he watched John nearly flip over the pile.

"Are you serious?!"

Ethan turned to head back toward the cabin. "That's what you get for cowardice."

"That's cold." John trotted to catch up to Ethan. "So, what did Beater say?"

Ethan rolled his eyes, knowing John was throwing random names out in malice. "He said he saw a car driving down the road yesterday. It's a one-way road that only accesses our homesteads. I think it was you, though. He also said he thought he saw someone up on the ridge where our properties connect, but he couldn't catch up to him." Ethan opened the door and stepped in. Rather than placing his rifle near the door, he kept it slung around his shoulder.

"He's going to put some more cameras up. Help keep an eye out for me."

"I'm somehow relieved by that."

"Doesn't matter. You need to get out, in case Vargas is out here. I don't want you getting caught up in the middle of that."

John plopped down on the couch, kicking his feet up onto the table. "Sorry, pal. I promised everyone I wouldn't go back until I knew you were okay. So I can either stay, or you can go with me, but those are the only options."

Ethan gave John a stern look. "Let's just pretend Vargas did find me. If I have to worry about you, it'll just get us both killed. I don't want that weight on my shoulders after..." His words trailed as an image of Kristina and Mary flashed in his mind. "After what I did to them."

"*You* didn't do anything. What happened to them was because of Vargas. You know that."

"I should've taken the threat more seriously. Because I didn't, they're dead. I won't make that mistake again."

John breathed out hard. He seemed more energized now, despite barely wanting to move just a half hour before. "I'll make you a deal. I'll only hang out until we know for sure it's just a random trespasser and not Vargas."

Ethan agreed reluctantly. "I'm going to bed. Tomorrow, we need to go to the river and try to gather some fish. Trout's in season."

"Thank God. Normal food."

Chapter 9

Ethan woke just before the sun. He was unsurprised to find John sprawled across the couch, snoring enthusiastically. He began going through his morning ritual, peering out of his window as the water boiled on the wood stove. His eyes methodically maneuvered across the woods outside. The snow had been substantially less than what had been predicted, yet more than he expected.

The snow was untouched. From his position at the window, he could see tracks of small game along two of the trails, but nothing that looked human.

Ethan had called the chief of IMPD a month ago. They still had no leads on Vargas. There had been an anonymous tip he was spotted in Mexico around August, but it was unsubstantiated. The CIs the police turned to when they needed answers on drug trafficking in Indianapolis reported they hadn't heard anything, but his operation was still running. They had also made it a point to remind Ethan he needed to keep a low profile until Vargas was captured.

Ethan gave up then. He succumbed to the fact the police would never find the man responsible for killing his family. He could never return to his old life without putting it in jeopardy, though, he didn't want to. He had grown to enjoy this simple life he had created. It was lonely. The guilt he felt for allowing Vargas to get to his family, stabbed at his mind relentlessly. His moment two nights before was one he had lived through more times than he could count over the past year. Just like every other time, he got through it.

Except this time, he thought he may have only gotten through it because John Waters had come to check on him. Had he answered one text or phone call, he might have taken the pills. He might not have. But he didn't answer them, and John did come. So, he lived, only to face the possibility of Vargas and his men having tracked him down. Forty-eight hours prior, he might not have cared. Now, that dark cloud had passed, and he did care.

Ethan's train of thought was broken by the piercing whistle of the kettle spout. He poured his coffee, letting the heat warm his palms. He went to the kitchen to retrieve his phone. No one had called or texted since John had arrived, so he assumed John had informed Ethan's mother he was alive and mostly well. He just hoped John hadn't told her how he was living. Or that someone had been sneaking onto the property.

Ethan's mother was pushing eighty. Ethan's leaving was the second significant loss in her life, coming just three years after his father had passed. His sister was still at home, hopefully caring for her. He would speak to his mother for a few minutes every week, but not nearly as often as he would have liked. He missed a lot of things about home, which John's presence only reminded him of more.

"I smell coffee," John groaned from the couch.

"Come get it," Ethan told him. "I'll cook up some eggs before we head down to the river."

"I thought you didn't go shopping?"

"There's a neighbor a couple of miles down the main road who sells them. I trade for them."

"What could you possibly have that anyone else would want?"

"Labor, venison, or scrap metal from the shed I tore down. There are a lot of things you can trade for out here. Most people try to be as self-sufficient as possible."

"As long as you have electricity, indoor plumbing, and a burner phone."

"Pretty much," Ethan raised his mug in a mocking toast. "How long has it been since you've gone fishing?" He asked to change the subject.

John's eyes squinted as he tried to recall. "Twenty-ish years. Never been trout fishing."

After Ethan cleaned up the dishes and they got dressed for the cool fall air, Ethan checked the chamber of his rifle by pulling the bolt back a few inches. Once satisfied, he pushed it forward and put the rifle on his back. "Fishing stuff is under the house." He said as if John cared one way or the other.

When he opened the door, something instantly caught his eye. He turned his attention to it; the sudden stop nearly caused John to run into him. "What the hell, man?"

"What is this?" Ethan asked rhetorically as he reached for the paper hanging from the door, tearing it from the nail that held it in place. "Did you hear anyone out here last night?"

Shock overwhelmed John's face. He only shook his head.

Ethan hadn't heard anyone either. Not even the nail being put into the door. The snow in front of the house was clear of prints, telling Ethan that, whoever had done it, did so before the snow came. They had to have been there between midnight and two in the morning. He wasn't surprised John had slept through the noise. The way the man snored he wouldn't hear an invading army blowing their trumpets in the middle of the living room. He was, however, surprised he hadn't heard it. He had always been a light sleeper, even more so since getting to the cabin.

Ethan examined the newspaper. It was the article covering the fire his family perished in. A red handprint was intentionally stamped to the front.

"At least they left prints," John choked out.

"They were wearing gloves," Ethan remarked, using his finger to point out the flatness of the marking.

"What does it mean?"

"There's blood on my hands. My family's blood." Ethan's throat tightened as something dark, something that frightened him, boiled in his chest.

"The blood is on his," John tried reminding him. "You were one of the best prosecutors the state ever had. This monster deserved to have you bury him. He may have gotten away once, but he won't again."

"We don't know where he is." He wadded up the paper, then threw it as hard as he could back into the house, only releasing an insignificant segment of his anger. "He proved last night he can get close to us anytime he wants. There isn't a damn thing we can do about it, either." His finger pointed back into the house. "That's what that paper proves."

John shook his head. "Now is exactly when you can get to him."

"How do you think that's even remotely possible? He nailed a paper to my door and neither one of us heard a damn thing."

"Because this isn't back home. People around here will notice someone like him wandering around. And there probably aren't a whole lot of places he can hide out here. A man like Vargas isn't going to hole up in the woods somewhere just to fuck with you."

Ethan considered this. "But his men would."

John shook his head. "This is personal, Ethan. One set of prints, one man spotted by Beaver, the paper on your front door. He's doing this one solo.

And Vargas would crash in a run-down motel before camping out in the woods."

"Okay," Ethan said. He knew what that meant, and he didn't like it. They were going to have to go into town. Something Ethan had done so seldom he could count his trips on one hand over the past year. "We might want to take Beaver. People will probably be more open to him than to me."

"You're one of them now, right?"

Ethan shook his head. "Beaver's been here decades. I've been here a year. And I've met three people."

"Well, I'm excited to finally get to meet the bear you call your neighbor."

"Go get in my truck."

John's face betrayed his hesitance. "We could take my BMW," he offered. "Better on gas."

"No one out here is going to be sharing much of anything with someone in a BMW. They'll already be on guard."

"Fine," he said reluctantly. "What about the police? We can stop by there, too. They'll probably be able to look in places we can't."

Ethan pulled his keys from his coat pocket and secured the door. "I don't want them involved."

"Why the hell not?"

"Because they will give the same story as Indy. They're going to work on it. They'll keep an eye out. By the time they get up to do anything, someone will already be dead."

"That's a bit melodramatic, don't you think?"

Ethan left the porch, walking toward his truck parked on the opposite side of John's BMW. "Is it? Because in the past year, all I was ever told was they had squat on getting justice for my family."

They got into the unlocked truck. Ethan flipped the visor down, catching the single key that fell from it.

"That isn't smart," John remarked.

"There isn't supposed to be anyone out here to try to steal it."

As Ethan put the key into the ignition, John's hand gripped his arm. The touch was cold. "Wait," John breathed. "In the movies, this would be a perfect time for a car bomb."

"You watch too many movies. Besides, you said yourself this was personal. Vargas wouldn't just blow me up."

Ethan started the truck, which choked for life. He began tapping the gas pedal with his foot, forcing the coughs to turn to growls, and then the engine roared with life. The Ford F-250 was something he bought when he officially moved into the cabin. An elderly man had it parked at the edge of his yard just outside of town. He figured it would be more useful out here than his Lexus. So, he sold the Lexus to a used car dealership, and bought the truck in cash, with plenty left over for the numerous repairs the thing needed. It ran reliably, though not well. Chunks of the body had rusted out, but the frame was still strong. Or so the mechanic had told him. He decided to believe him because he didn't have enough left over to buy another one.

"Let me do all the talking with Beaver. He's a little jumpy, he might not like me bringing a stranger around."

John shrugged. "It's your call."

Chapter 10

"It sounds like he is even more of a hermit than you. What makes you think he'll help you?"

Ethan shot a side-eye toward John. He drove slowly down the one-mile between his cabin and Beaver's, careful not to shake anything loose under the truck. "It's his code."

"His code?"

"When I first got here, he came over and introduced himself. Kind of. Took me hunting for the first time. He told me part of his code was to be a good neighbor. The fact I hardly ever see him makes me think he sticks to that pretty well."

"But if you get him involved, you're going to have to tell him about your past. Or have you already shared that with him?"

Ethan swallowed through a flutter. "Not really a casual conversation topic." Ethan watched as some red and orange leaves danced toward the gravel road in front of him. Kristina and Mary always loved the fall. They used to go to Brown County just before Halloween every year when the leaves were at their peak beauty. In the city, views like that didn't exist. Even in their neighborhood, trees were a commodity. Mary got to jump in leaves only once a year.

Ethan pulled himself from the thought as he turned down the narrow drive, which was uneven and riddled with craters. He drove up a quarter mile, which would end at the house. But the trees were growing close to the drive, which was precarious at best. Limbs reached for his truck. When he was at the cabin—which he realized then he had never been to—he took notice of how differently Beaver lived than he.

The cabin was a two-story wooden structure that almost looked like it was being renovated, but Ethan suspected it just needed the work rather than there being a plan to ever do it. Ethan guessed that tarps had been strung across portions of the second floor to slow water damage. The yard, which was not as open as Ethan's, was littered with scrap metal and wood. A leaning shed sat behind the house, and a makeshift wooden support was pressed to the leaning side to prevent further damage.

"No," John said. "This screams *Deliverance*."

"You're an asshole sometimes, you know that?"

"This man barely has a hold of his own life. You think *he* is the best option for help?" John's eyes were scolding.

"I don't know if he is the best. But he is the only."

John turned frustrated, "Except for perhaps the police."

"I don't trust the police to do anything. Are you coming or not?"

"I guess so. Even if he doesn't kill you, something in his junkyard sure might."

Ethan let the comment go. They got out of the truck—which Ethan left running out of fear it may not start when they got back—and went straight for the front door. Beaver had orchestrated a clear path that allowed access to the door.

"There're no other vehicles here. Are you sure he's even home?"

Ethan had noticed no trucks were parked around the house; he had thought very little of it. "Some people park behind their houses. He has a lot of land so he may have a second entry spot. Besides I've never seen or heard a car come from this way. For all I know, he doesn't drive."

After navigating the precarious porch, they reached the front door. A third of the wood beneath them had been replaced in patches, a third was rotten and crumbling, and the other third was waiting its turn to disintegrate. Ethan waited a few seconds after his first knock before trying again.

"I don't think he's here," John sighed, mildly relieved.

"Beaver!" Ethan shouted with his hands cupped around his mouth.

John looked around as if expecting the call to suddenly summon the man from nowhere.

"We'll wait a minute then just head into town. I bet you scared him away with your city-folkness."

"City-folkness? Pretty sure that's not a real thing," John scoffed.

"Well, it is now." Ethan scanned the woods, which, from his position, mainly lay hidden behind the piles of scraps. "Maybe we'll try again later. I think there's a couple of places we can ask around yet where his presence might not be needed."

They drove down State Road 35, navigating the switchbacks that still had spots of snow and ice. The normally fifteen-minute drive had taken nearly twenty-five. The Hillside Motel sat a mile outside the main part of Bakerville, Indiana. In its heyday, the motel was probably a nice place. Now, the building looked like it should've been condemned sometime in the previous decade.

The tall neon sign outside the building, which boasted the motel's name, whether there was a vacancy, and the fact they had HBO had long since burned out with no plans to repair. The only light that still flickered on the sign was the *V* in vacancy. The building looked as though it had been all white at one point. Now, it was a stained beige color with red doors along the outside, most of which had missing spots of paint.

The main office, where Ethan parked the truck, stuck out twenty feet from the rest of the building. It had wrap-around windows that ended where the office and motel met. Even from the truck, Ethan could tell the lighting inside cast out a harsh yellow hue, which made everything else look smoke-stained.

Ethan turned the truck off, preferring a fight to get it started than risking it being stolen. Only half a dozen other cars lined the face of the motel, parked in front of various rooms. He suspected some people were renting by the week or month despite regulations against it. He had seen it a lot in the city; old motels desperate to keep an inflow of cash would allow people to rent long-term. Almost always, those tenants used it as their drug hole. Either to sell or use. A place like this may have been below Vargas' standards, but he would certainly feel right at home.

"What's the plan?" John asked, following Ethan to the entrance of the decaying motel.

"I'll ask if he's seen Vargas and see what he says."

"I doubt he would be using his real name," John pointed out.

"Doesn't matter. I have a picture of him on my phone."

John looked uneased by the comment. "Why?"

"So I don't forget the face of the man who killed my family."

John nodded, saying nothing. Ethan opened the door and went in. A man with the body structure of a child and the face of neglected leather sat behind the desk. A half-smoked cigarette dangled from his chapped lips.

"Hour, night, or week?" The man huffed through the cigarette. His voice scratched at the ears when he spoke. The man reached below the desk, retrieving a pair of glasses he put on, and a clipboard he slid across the desk toward Ethan and

John. He looked up at the two, an uninterested flatness in his eyes.

"Well," Ethan said, putting his phone down on the counter. "I was wondering if this man has checked in recently?"

"Are you a cop?"

"Do we look like cops?" John asked.

"I don't think so," Ethan offered. "We're just curious if our friend checked in. He was supposed to meet up with us last evening and didn't show up. This is the closest motel around."

The man gave him a curious look. "That new Hilton fifteen miles out past the pumpkin farm ain't too far." The man gave Ethan a once-over. "If he's like you, that'd probably be more his style." Ethan smirked, "He likes to rough it."

The man took a flustered breath in, coughing over the sudden increase in smoke. He finally removed the cigarette from his lips, laying it on top of the desk.

"Just take a look," John grumbled.
The man leaned over the phone, looking at the picture upside down. Ethan rotated it for him and pushed it in closer. "Don't look familiar. Seems like someone I'd recognize."

"Is it possible someone else may have checked him in?"

The man moved his head rapidly, looking around the room with his arms raised. "Do it look like I can afford to hire anyone else? It's just me."

"Thank you for your time," Ethan said.

"You were very helpful," John mocked.

"Uh-huh," the man brought the cigarette back to his lips, letting the smoke dance around his face. Once back outside, John asked, "So, now what?"

"Let's sit in the truck and watch the place for a bit. See if Vargas comes or goes?"

"If he does, then what? We're not going to confront him ourselves."

"No," Ethan agreed. "Then we will call the cops. At least then, we know he's here, and they can finally put an end to this."

"What if he doesn't show up?" John got into the truck, foregoing the seatbelt.

"Then we stop by the Hilton. You might as well look up the directions on your phone?"

"What's wrong with your phone?" John complained even as he was retrieving his phone.

"That burns up a lot of data on a pre-paid phone. I'd rather not use it all in one day."

Ethan adjusted his rear-view mirror to catch anyone pulling into the parking lot. He then positioned himself in the front seat to be able to maintain a direct view of the few cars already there. He would see anyone coming or going. There was one dark-colored car that looked better cared for than the rest. A 2019 Acura, which seemed too reserved for Vargas. Ethan guessed that if he wanted to blend in, he would know to choose something non-descript. The car had been backed into its space so he couldn't read the license plate.

He would sit there for ten minutes before moving on. He already felt suspicious. He didn't need to draw any more attention to himself.

Chapter 11

After nearly fifteen minutes, Ethan turned on the truck. They turned right out of the motel, heading toward Melford, where they would take another right. At County Road 15, they would go left, following that the rest of the way to the Hilton Hotel. It sat just two miles outside of Shelby, a small college community of only 5,000 residents. Most of them were students at Triton University.

The rancid motel was less than half the distance from his cabin than the Hilton. As he thought about it, it made less sense that Vargas would have been staying there. He would have wanted to stay close, in case Ethan moved. But they were already on the way.

Without thought, Ethan spoke, "She wasn't supposed to be home that day, you know?"

John didn't speak for a moment. Then asked for clarification, "Who?"

"Mary. She was supposed to be in preschool. I texted Kristina I was going to get her on my way home because I got out early. When I got to the school, they told me she had stayed home sick."

"I'm sorry, Ethan. I didn't know that."

"I think Kristina kept her home because she was tired. If I had done more, Kristina wouldn't have felt so overwhelmed and she would've been on her way to get Mary."

"You can't assume that. Maybe Mary really was out sick, it wouldn't have mattered what you did. There's nothing you could've done differently to change what happened."

Ethan glanced over doubtfully at John. "You might be right. But it could've been different if Kristina knew she could count on me to be on time. Kristina sometimes kept Mary home during afternoon meetings because it was only preschool. She couldn't always end her meetings in time to get her." Ethan choked through the emotion threatening to expose itself. "If I had been more reliable, she wouldn't have had to worry about it."

"And if Vargas wasn't such a waste of life, none of that would matter. He was going to go after you no matter what. Even if it wasn't that day, it would've been soon."

"I could've offered him a better deal. You know we didn't have any hard evidence he was even transporting the drugs? And the attempted murder and kidnapping charges were about to be dropped. The witness and victim were already pulling out."

John shifted in his seat. "Then why did he care what you were charging him with? He already got to the two people who could put him away."

Ethan no longer felt like talking. He knew why Vargas had put a target on him. The target was there whether he followed through with the case or not. But, he thought, if he had done things differently, he could've saved his family. There was no solace in that, however. No matter what, he would not let himself off the hook. He couldn't stop blaming himself; it wouldn't be fair to show himself grace. "Forget it. I just want to find this sonofabitch and end this. It can only end when one or both of us are dead."

John's eyes showed his unease.

Once they parked, John pointed out the sign advertising a pub in the hotel. "We should start there."

"Why?"

"Because if the motel guy cared about customer privacy, I guarantee the front desk here will. Waiters don't have the same standards."

"The other guy didn't care. He just wanted to extort us for money."

John nodded, "These guys won't. They just won't talk to us. And unlike that motel, they'll be fine calling the cops. Do you want that?"

Ethan shook his head. "What makes you think the restaurant staff will know Vargas? Or hell, that they'll even talk if they do?"

"If he's staying here, he has to eat. This is convenient. A man like Vargas sticks out. Someone will recognize him if he's been here."

"That's smart," Ethan agreed. "I guess you can be useful when you want to be."

"Since you're so open to advice right now, we could also just go back to the cabin, pack up, head home, and tell IMPD Vargas found you. Let them deal with it."

"And there, you lost it."

"Then let's go."

The restaurant was less upscale than Ethan had expected from a Hilton. Despite that, he still felt himself being self-conscious about how he looked walking in. His dirty jeans and stained flannel shirt made him stand out. His hair was wild, he was sure, and the unkempt beard on his face wasn't even trimmed. John at least looked like he belonged.

The area sanctioned for the restaurant had fresh white paint on all the walls. Windows had been spaced every five feet, allowing diners to get a direct view of the Triton University football field surrounded by other buildings on campus. A long empty bar was to the left of the 'Seat Yourself' sign. Square tables were scattered throughout the dining area, and white tablecloths were used to complement the white walls.

"I'd hate to see their cleaning bill," Ethan mused, trying to take his mind off how little he belonged there.

"It's a write-off."

Ethan and John made their way to a table off to the right, away from the bar where people were more likely to sit. They had just enough time to open the menu before a man in his early twenties approached them with a rehearsed smile.

"Hi, my name is Geoff. I'll be your waiter today. Would you like to start with a drink?"

"I'll just take a water," Ethan said, looking at John, who nodded in agreement. "Two."
The waiter nodded. As he turned to grab the drinks, Ethan stopped him.

"Excuse me, I'm looking for a friend of mine who said he has been staying here. He was supposed to meet us for lunch."

"I haven't seen anyone since breakfast. What does he look like?"

"Latino man. He has a scar over his left eye and always wears his hair slicked back like James Bond."

"And he's always chewing on a toothpick," John added.

Geoff thought for a moment. "Doesn't sound familiar, but between school and here, I see so many faces they all start to run together." A second thought entered his mind. "There's a lot of bars and stuff near campus. Maybe he wanted to meet there?"

"I guess we'll pass on the water and see if he went somewhere else."

"If you know his room number, I can see if he's put in a room service order."

"I know his name. Vargas?"

"Just a moment." Geoff turned from the table and vanished behind a set of double doors.

"How many fugitives do you know who check into hotels using their real names?" John asked facetiously.

"I don't exactly have a Rolodex of all his aliases."

Geoff emerged from the double doors, going straight to their table. "No such luck," he told them. "Sorry."

Ethan pulled his wallet from his pocket and opened it. He only operated in cash, but even still, carried very little. He pulled his last five-dollar bill from the middle and handed it to Geoff. "Thank you for your help. We'll see if he meant for us to meet him somewhere else."

Once outside, John asked, "Are we really going to go to every bar and eatery in town?"

"Of course not. We're going back to the cabin to see if the cameras tell us anything. If I can figure out where he's coming in from or leaving to, it'll be easier to cut him off next time. Bring the fight to him."

"That's a real shame," John sighed. "I could go for a drink."

Chapter 12

When they returned to the cabin, Ethan wondered if Beaver had stopped by. He wondered if the old-timer had spotted the unwelcomed visitor wondering the land again.

Ethan parked the pickup and told John to go inside and pour some drinks, saying he would be inside after collecting the cards from the cameras. He hadn't brought his rifle with him on their fruitless expedition, a decision he'd regretted when they arrived at the rancid motel. Rather than going in to grab it, he bent over to grab a large stick from the ground. It mainly felt dry despite the recent flurries, and it felt sturdy. He could use it if he needed to.

More leaves had fallen since the day before, leaving some of the treetops almost entirely bare. It also came with another problem. The earth beneath the leaves, as well as the leaves themselves, were damp from the quarter inch of snow. Since it had melted, the leaves would not only cover the ground, hiding any tracks of an unwanted visitor, but they would also stifle the sound of someone walking. Out here, Ethan had learned that the best way to keep ahead of his prey was to be able to locate them. He was getting better at tracking their prints and at hearing them before they saw him so that he could adjust for the best shots.

He started with the two cameras John had set up, but couldn't find them. They were not where Ethan told him to place them, allowing one the perfect angle toward the house and the other toward the vehicles. He walked quickly to the woodpile where John had been hiding the night before, assuming John had heard Ethan's therapeutic yell before he had hung them. But he didn't see them there, either. Those cameras could have shown who put the paper on the door, or if they had put a tracker on either car.

Ethan huffed a furious sigh at the ineptitude. Both John's and his own. If he had thought to check the cameras after finding the newspaper nailed to his door, he would have known hours ago that the cameras hadn't been set. He was angry John had fumbled his one task so completely, but the frustration he had for himself was stronger.

Ethan trudged up the hill behind his cabin to collect the cards from the cameras he had set up. He collected his cards, keeping his eyes open toward the surrounding woods every step of the way. Every fallen tree, boulder, and mound of leaves could have been a spot where someone could conceal themselves.

When he descended the hill toward the ravine to collect his final card, he spotted something that caught his attention. Three trees over was one of his other cameras—one of the cameras John was supposed to have set. It peered directly at him. His frustration at John's ineptness grew hotter. His friend was going to get them both killed. He had explicitly told John where to set cameras, and the ravine was not one of them. Either he intentionally ignored him, or he was stupid.

Then Ethan wondered why he would intentionally ignore him. The man wasn't stupid. He was a lawyer. A damn good one. He graduated in the top 20 of his class, aced the Bar, and he knew how to follow directions. He also knew not to take chances with a man like Vargas. So, more than likely, John had intentionally set the camera in that specific location. And he had done it sometime after Ethan left to go up the hill, where he ended up running into Beaver. From there, he could have run straight up the small graded hill to the cabin, saw Beaver, then ducked under the front porch to hide under the woodpile. Ethan pushed the thoughts aside, not wanting to waste time on hyperbole when he had cards to check.

"I couldn't find the alcohol," John said as Ethan entered, tossing the camera cards onto the table. Ethan walked over to the cabinet to retrieve the bottle of Jack Daniels. "I have six cabinets and a fridge. It isn't hard to look."

John caught the edge of Ethan's tone. "Did something happen out there?"

"Not sure," he said, looking at John, gauging whether he seemed nervous or not. "Where did you set the cameras last night?"

"Exactly where you told me to," he said flatly. There was no raising or lowering in the timbre of his voice, which Ethan knew meant John was confident in what he was saying. "One near my car and one on the other side pointed at the house."

"Then why did I only find one? And it was down in the ravine where I told you I was setting a camera?"

John's eyebrows raised as he shook his head. "Couldn't tell you. I put them where you said and pushed the button you told me to. Then I heard you scream, went to the side of the house when I saw you talking with Beaver. Then I hid."
The question Ethan wanted to ask—but didn't—hung at the tip of his tongue. *How do I know I can trust you?*

He swallowed the words, opening his laptop instead of speaking. John rounded the table to lean over Ethan's shoulder. Ethan felt them tense as he did. He went through the cards from his two cameras, spotting only a few small game animals, one doe, and a falling leaf.

Then he inserted the card from John's camera, which had over a dozen photos. But he noticed instantly that they were not marked the same as the camera's normally marked photos. Typically, the camera would provide a sequence of ten numbers that seemed to follow no particular order. These photos were marked with four digits. The capture dates also didn't make sense. Ethan was confident he had cleared the cards before putting them back into the cameras; however, this one had photos dating back two days.

"What's wrong?" John asked, clearly picking up on the tightening of Ethan's body.

Ethan had been clenching his teeth so tightly, they began to ache. He cleared his throat before speaking. "I don't think this is our card."

"What does that mean? Whose card is it?"

"I don't know. But it isn't set up like it normally is. And there shouldn't be this many photos after less than twenty-four hours."

"Well, open it."

"It could have a virus."

"You're not connected to the internet, are you?"

"No," Ethan glanced down at the right corner of his laptop to verify, even though he knew he didn't have internet at the cabin.

"Then open it."

Chapter 13

Each picture Ethan scanned through was a chilling reminder of how vulnerable he was despite the precautions he thought he had taken. He had never set his cabin up as a fortress. He never thought he'd need to. Every section around the cabin had some sort of vulnerability. Yet it was startling just how close Vargas had gotten to him without detection. He was further fueling the gut feeling that John had led Vargas right to him.

Of the 20 photos, the last few were the most concerning. The first several were from the ridge with a telescoping lens, allowing the photographer to get an up-close view of the cabin through the bare treetops. He couldn't know for sure, but it looked like it could be near the area where Beaver claimed to have seen someone, and around the same timeframe. However, Beaver hadn't mentioned the intruder carrying anything, which would have been odd.

When he was an intern, Ethan did a stakeout one night with a private investigator for a case. The equipment was bulky and quite heavy, and a large bag was required to carry it all around. Whatever Vargas was using was likely much more significant than what the investigator used.

The next set of photos was of Ethan's cabin, him walking around the property. They were much closer than the previous set, shot from the ridge, within a hundred yards easily.

The final set of photos had been of Ethan's truck outside the motel and the hotel. These were so close that the guy had to be in the same parking lot—close enough that had Ethan seen him, he could've seen the taunting in his eyes.

"I told you, you lead him right to me," Ethan growled.

Without defense, John said, "How do you know this is even Vargas? Further, how do you know he wasn't already here?"

"Am I supposed to just think it's a coincidence the day you arrive is the day all this shit starts?"

"If he trailed me, how did he park and get to the ridge to take those photos? Navigating the woods and getting to the right spot would take some planning. And, how could he take those photos at the hotel and still get back here to put them in the trail thing, then leave, before we got back?"

Ethan considered that. "He could have brought someone with him."

"You need to think back to that day in court, where all of this really started."

Ethan wondered what made John think that was when it had started. Instead of asking, he told him, "I remember everything about that day. I could never forget anything about it. It started the worst time of my life!"

"You remember the big things," John told him. "One of the partners I knew always said, 'People remember the big things. But they never remember the millions of minute details.'"

John sat down next to Ethan. "If he is working with someone, they may've been in the courtroom that day. Try to remember anyone he might've talked to. He could've slipped someone something."

"How am I supposed to remember that? That was a year ago."

"Well, we know he isn't working with a team. He knows that would be too conspicuous out here. And too much overkill. He isn't doing it alone. So, who else could be helping him?"

Ethan had the nagging urge to shout, *You!* But he bit his tongue. John had been his best friend for years, one of the few people he could count on. Plus, he reminded himself, if they had something big enough on John to get him to turn, they would've done it months ago. He closed his eyes, taking a deep breath to suppress the invading thought.

"Okay, John. I'll try. But it still doesn't help us. We don't know where they are coming in from, and what's worse is that they are getting closer. Which means they're getting more comfortable. They're going to make their move soon."

"Then I guess you can either run, again. Or you can do something about it."

"I'll try to remember something. I just don't think it'll be any more helpful than the nothing we have right now."

John shrugged. "You could always shave your beard, wash your hair, and go on the move. No one would recognize you."

Ethan shook his head, slamming the laptop closed. "I'm tired of hiding."

Chapter 14

The night seemed to linger as Ethan lay restless in bed. He had tried to sleep for hours but each turn introduced a new lump in the mattress he had never noticed. If he happened to find a semi-comfortable position, his legs would want to move. His heart thumped an unusual beat—though not all that unfamiliar if he thought about it. Ethan's mind refused to slow, going from one thought to another, yet never to the place he knew it should be.

John had been right, as much as Ethan hated to remember it. There were probably things he had forgotten about the day Vargas was pulled from court. He shifted again, finding a comfortable position. He thought he might be able to lay still long enough to search his memory.

The court was primarily empty. Less than a handful of reporters were there to document the proceedings of a low-end cartel leader being tried for trafficking, murder, racketeering, and a handful of other charges. The police had handed Ethan a mountain of evidence, which he carved and crafted into a presentable art piece to show a jury. Like how Gutzon Bolgrum transformed Six Grandfather's Mountain into Mount Rushmore.

Vargas had flown under the radar for decades, content with allowing his competition to take up most of the typeface of the headlines. As they began to fall, he took the opportunity to expand. It had been by dumb luck the police got him at all. He had been with two other guys passing through Indiana on a cross-country trip from Georgia to Illinois. The Crossroads of America made transporting efficient. Except Vargas's tire blew on I-65 North. Two state troopers stopped to help when they started catching bullets from one of Vargas's hot-headed and eager-to-impress accomplices. Six hours and two shoot-outs later, Vargas was in custody, already planning his brutality lawsuit, despite two state troopers losing their lives.

Judge Atkins started. He was a burly man who wore his battle scars proudly. His time in the Marines was viewed as a higher accomplishment than his time behind the bench. He was hard-nosed on crime, which usually worked in Ethan's favor. He clung to the few strands of gray still visible on his head as he clung to his oath to uphold the law. Unlike Ethan, who found interpretation important, he didn't play loose with it. He ran through the litany of charges, then asked, "How do you plead?"

"No culpable," Vargas said in Spanish. Ethan knew the man spoke fluent English. But it was an excellent tactic to draw out proceedings.

"Not guilty," his lawyer, whom Ethan didn't know, reiterated. The woman representing Angel

Vargas was attractive and confident, but clearly out of her element. She looked to be only a few years out of law school, making this—most likely—her first big case. "We are in the process of working out a deal," she told the court.

Atkins's face showed his contempt. His eyes scolded her for the comment before moving to Ethan, scolding him for even considering it.

"Is this true, Mr. Barret?"

"It is, Judge. We are finalizing some of the details, but we are happy with the terms."

"What are those terms, exactly?" Atkins leaned his heavy body onto his elbows, scowling down at Ethan.

His stomach flipped like when he was a child, caught by his parents doing something he knew he wasn't supposed to. "Ten years in a federal prison. Ten years of probation after."

The judge looked down at a sheet of paper in front of him. "Mr. Vargas was involved in two police shootings in which four officers were hit in the line of duty. Two were killed, leaving a wife and two young children without a husband and father. He started a six-hour chase and manhunt, endangering the lives of countless citizens. He was found in possession with the intent to distribute more controlled substances than most hospitals carry.

"How do you have the audacity to stand before this court and tell everyone present ten years is a sentence you are happy with? I am not happy with that, Mr. Barret." Judge Atkins turned his attention to Vargas and his lawyer. "I am going to deny this plea, as I believe justice will not be served in its acceptance."

Ethan's heart stopped. His stomach went from flipping to clenching, nearly dropping him to his knees. He didn't need to see Vargas to know how he had taken the decision.

"No! We made a deal!" His accent, though thick, didn't conceal the rage in his message, which Ethan heard clearly. "You will pay for this!"

Ethan somehow managed to move his eyes toward Vargas as he continued the tirade. "You're dead," Vargas screamed in Ethan's direction. He knew the message was meant for him. "Everything you've ever loved will be burned to the ground!"

"You are in contempt," Atkins shouted over his slamming hammer. "Get him out of here!"

Ethan watched the bailiff and two Sherrif's Department deputies drag him from his seat toward a set of doors to the right of the judge. Before they pulled him from the table, he managed to contort his body enough to toss a wadded paper over the rails into the gallery. A man in his early twenties, one of the few people sitting on his side of the courtroom, leaned over to grab the ball before anyone noticed.

With all the commotion, no one had. Even Ethan hadn't noticed. He was too focused on what had just happened. His life and career flashed before his eyes.

Ethan stood from his bed and went directly to his closet, which held four outfits and a box containing the last remnants of his old life. After tugging on the chain to light the small area, he kneeled in front of the box, opened it, and retrieved the object at the top.

It was a charred teddy bear. The only thing that survived the blaze, Ethan felt was worth keeping. He had given it to Mary on her first birthday. From then on, it lived in the crevices of her arm. She had been holding it when the fireman pulled her from her room. It was in her arms when they strapped her to the gurney and rushed her to the hospital.

Ethan realized he was sobbing only when he found he was struggling to breathe.

He returned the bear to its place in the box, forcing himself to his feet, knowing he wasn't going to be getting any sleep that night. The sun would be rising in less than half an hour, and in either case, it was a losing situation for him. If he managed to get some sleep, he knew, he would only dream of Mary and Kristina, of him trying to get to them in the intensity of the flames. Failing every time. He would sleep into the late morning, leaving him vulnerable and unaware when someone would most likely be coming onto his property. He would be leaving John unsupervised access to everything.

He pinched the bridge of his nose, trying to redirect his thoughts and suppress the headache that was forming behind his eyes.

Ethan looked to his window just as a dark blob passed by. It took a moment for what he had seen to register in his mind. Once it did, he grabbed his rifle from the foot of his bed, where he stood, and then ran out into the late October night, wearing only his shorts.

Chapter 15

The darkness wrapped around Ethan as he burst into the coldness of the night. He had called for John when he sprinted through the living room, but John hadn't seemed to notice. The sun kissed the horizon, casting a soft blue glow over the tree line, but it did little to help Ethan see where the figure had gone. It was far too big to be a deer.

He turned his focus to the left when he heard the snapping of a twig. The silhouette appeared smaller than it had when passing by his window. Of course, now he was more awake. More alert. The figure ran across his lawn near the road, heading for the tree line. He had one shot, or the intruder would break into the woods and be gone.

Ethan raised his rifle, pressing the butt of the stock hard into his shoulder. He knew it was too dark for the scope to be of any use. He also knew that he wouldn't need to hit his target. He hoped if Vargas, or whomever he had sent, knew he had heavy firepower, they would stop coming around for a while. Giving him enough time to secure his land properly.

Ethan lined his barrel up a few yards in front of where the shadowy figure was running. He squeezed the trigger firmly. Instead of the deafening clap he expected, there was a heart-stopping and defeating metallic click.

Ethan rotated his rifle to the left so he could see the safety switch on the right, near the trigger guard. The safety was off, showing a round red circle, confirming it was ready to fire. He cursed himself for not making sure there was a round in the chamber. He pulled the bolt back and then slammed it forward as forcefully as he could. Ethan noticed the brass of a round eject from the rifle, but he didn't have time to think about that. Ethan then raised his rifle again for another shot. When he did, his target was gone.

Ethan watched the woods for a moment, disappointed they had vanished. Ethan scanned the grass for a shimmer of the brass, found it poking through a weed, and retrieved it. He checked the back, noting that the firing pin had been punctured. He flipped the round to inspect the bullet, which was gone.

He thought back to the last time he had fired the rifle. It had been the evening he shot the deer. Ethan distinctly remembered putting a new round in the chamber in case the deer wasn't dead when he approached it. Someone had replaced the bullet in the chamber with a dummy round.

Why? Who?

Ethan pulled the bolt back again, ensuring there was a live round. Satisfied there was, he stormed back into the house, his rifle pointing forward.

As soon as he entered, he spotted John exiting the bathroom mid-yawn, his hands over his eyes. When John saw Ethan, he asked, "What were you doing out there?"

Ethan didn't speak. Instead, he rushed John, who was too close to sleep to react. Ethan raised the stock of his rifle, pressing it into John's neck. Ethan drove John backward into the wall. The sturdy wood wall made no noise and had no give as the two men collided into it.

"Was it you?" Ethan demanded to know. "Did you change my bullets?"

"You know it wasn't. I wouldn't even know how to swap bullets." John's hands pressed against the stock of the rifle, just enough to not suffocate.

"Someone was outside and when I took a shot, my gun misfired. Turns out, someone replaced my bullet with a dummy round."

"What the hell are you even talking about?"

"Why were you not here when I woke up? I yelled for you. Where the hell were you?" Ethan's eyes narrowed, his mind telling him John Waters was part of all of this.

"I was taking a leak, Ethan. If I was outside, how could I have gotten back to the cabin and in through the window before you got back?" He pressed more firmly against the stock. Ethan pressed back. "All this is making you paranoid. Why would I want to do anything to you?"

Ethan pushed his face closer to John's, making sure he was close to his eyes so he could catch a tell. "We both know you have expensive tastes in women and a problem walking away from the card table. Vargas could easily buy you."

"A lot has changed in the past year, Ethan. Neither of us is the same man. I haven't gambled once."

Ethan eased his weight off the rifle.

John raised his head to stretch his neck. "You have no one else. You have to trust me. I'm not conspiring against you, I didn't sell you out, and I sure as hell didn't intentionally lead anyone out here. I'm in this just the same as you."

Ethan took a deep breath, slowing the nagging thoughts in his mind that refused to stop.

"We were gone most of the day yesterday. Anyone could've gotten into the house and swapped that round."

"Maybe," Ethan admitted.

"What do you know about your neighbor? He knew you weren't home."

"I know he has no idea who I am, no idea who Angel Vargas is, and has no need for money. He's even more of a recluse than I am."

"Who says he doesn't have his reasons for wanting you gone?"

Ethan stepped away from John, turning toward the couch where he sat. The radiant warmth of the wood stove hit his bare legs and feet, relaxing him slightly. "Because I've been here a year. If he wanted me gone, he has had ample time to do it. He even took me hunting. If a man wants to kill another man, being alone in the woods with a gun is a great time to do it."

John stood in the kitchen, keeping his distance. "We might've jumped the line on thinking it was Vargas."

"There is one man on this planet that would want to kill me. It sounds like you're trying to put doubt of that in my head. Not putting much more confidence in me."

John raised his hands in surrender. "I'm just saying, we need to consider everyone. Vargas is obvious. Your neighbor could want more land or feel like you're encroaching on his way of life. One of Vargas's associates could want to retaliate."

John considered his own words for a moment. "Didn't you attack one of his guys?"

"I don't know," Ethan said, burying his face in his hands. His life had already been flipped upside-down once. He didn't know how he could handle it happening again. He also wondered what it was that made him care at all. Just days ago, he was ready to end his life. He began to wonder if it would be easier to just let fate take care of itself. But then, what about John? He wasn't sure if he could trust him, but there was a guilt with the thought. John may have been the one person he did trust. Ethan wasn't a therapist, but he wondered if he had hoped he could just push John away, to be left alone in solitude. To let things end the way he wanted them to.

"I think we should consider all possible angles."

"Yeah," was all Ethan said before standing up, grabbing his rifle, and heading back to his room.

Chapter 16

Ethan stared out his window as the sun broke the crest of the woods, casting a warm yellow ray over his lawn. Even for late October, he could tell it was going to be a rare day when he wouldn't need his coat. He also knew that it wouldn't last. Snow was coming later in the evening, more than the dusting they had before. He had a lot of wood to collect still, food to prep, but he realized he wasn't going to get the chance. Vargas—or if John was right, whoever—was out there with them— was getting more brazen. It was only a matter of time before he did what he was there to do.

John's words circled in his mind, trailing vague images of Vargas's associates. The man he only just remembered from the trial. The man in the precinct. Pictures the FBI and DEA had taken of Vargas talking to various people. Some of equal power, but most with less. He recognized none of them, and if they stood before him, then he wouldn't recognize them either. Except for the man he attacked in the IMPD precinct three hours after his family had been slain.

He was there to look through mugshots, despite his repeated—and unheard—arguments pointing to Vargas. A neighbor had even told them they had seen someone walking through the neighborhood who matched Vargas' description. The only thing the police ever said was, "We are looking into him as a possibility."

Vargas had made bail just days after his court outburst because the feds probably only found a fraction of his blood money. Two days after he made bail, Ethan's house was torched. No one saw Vargas after that.

The closest Ethan got to Vargas was sitting at the desk of Detective Richard Reinbolt, the man in charge of his family's case. He was showing Ethan a slew of mugshots of people who also matched the description given by the neighbor, except they didn't. A uniformed officer pushed a man down the hall, his hands cuffed behind his back. Ethan instantly recognized him as a co-defendant, Manuel Rodrigez, who was being tried separately from Vargas. Ethan had worked closely with the Assistant DA working that case, so the man's face had been etched in his memory.

Ethan lost what little control he had left in that moment. His sight went red, and his skin burned despite the cold sweat beading from every pore. He left his body, floating above himself. It was as if he were watching his movements from a screen somewhere else. Each movement was weightless, as if he floated through the air, almost like a dream, except he knew it wasn't.

Ethan erupted from the chair, causing it to flip on its side. He raced toward the cuffed Manuel. The officers reached for him, but it was like they reached through him. His foot found the top of a desk as he sailed over a computer and into Manuel, taking them both and the uniformed officer to the ground.

Hands were grabbing him, pulling at him; pepper spray had been deployed, but the swarm of officers may as well not have been there at all. Ethan rained fists down on Manuel, and new gashes opened each time. Then, without conscious thought, he grabbed Manuel's collar. He could hear the man's head hitting the floor, but it sounded distant. In the chaos, nothing held any reality to him. Sounds were dulled, almost inaudible entirely. His vision blending from red to black.

The next thing he knew he was coming to in a jail cell. It felt as though his head were three times its standard size, a speaker playing crashing thunder seemed to have been placed right by his ear. When he vomited, he realized the noise was coming from inside his head. Every part of his body ached, but none as much as his lower back and his fists. His muscles felt like Jello, so he didn't dare try to stand. He called out to the empty hall, then had to silence himself before throwing up again.

"That was a real shit show," Detective Reinbolt said coming down the hall.

Ethan squinted his eyes to keep the light out. "What happened?"

"You don't remember?" Reinbolt leaned against the cell with one hand. His suit was an off-the-rack from J.C. Penny, a polar opposite of Ethan's. He chomped down on some gum, which Ethan knew was intended to help him cut his twenty-year pack-a-day habit. It was annoying, but it seemed to work.

"I was looking at pictures... Rodrigez came in... That's all I remember."

"You damn near killed the man. Took eight officers to restrain you. You know you're facing some serious problems with this, and you might have fucked up your case. We were going to interview him about your house and Vargas." Reinbolt put his face to Ethan's cage, his eyes stern. "Now, he's in a hospital bed with tubes down his throat and a hole in his skull to stop the swelling. You might've cost us our one shot."

Ethan began sobbing, making every roaring ache in his body scream. It didn't bother him. Not like Reinbolt's words. "I let them down again. I promised them I would always protect them."

Reinbolt's eyes softened then. "Look, you went through a lot. I think anyone in your position would've lost it too. Especially knowing what kind of man Rodrigez is. I don't think you'll face any time, but there must be consequences."

Ethan choked back the pain. "Doesn't matter what happens to me."

"You've done a lot of good for this city, Barret." He pulled his gum from his mouth, replacing it with a new piece and wrapping the used gum in the wrapper. "It might be a good idea for you to think about going away for a while until everything is worked out. I'll stay in contact as things unfold. We'll get 'im."

Two months later, Ethan was in the cabin. Reinbolt called a lot less often. He knew Rodrigez had some permanent damage from the attack, but he was a free man. He also had reason to want payback. Either he and Vargaz were working together, or he had his help. Both seemed just as likely, though he wondered how probable it was either man would waste time rather than just killing him.

Unless they wanted him to know how much more power they had than him.

Ethan was pulled from his thoughts by a knock at his bedroom door. He locked the memories back into a dark corner of his mind. "Yeah?"

Chapter 17

John opened the door before he leaned against the frame, "Are we good?"

Ethan's body relaxed slightly before he offered a simple grin.

"I was thinking, if you really aren't sure you can trust me, I can leave. I don't want you having to worry about these guys *and* me," he gave a half-smirk. "I would prefer you to come along so I don't have to worry about you. But I get it either way."

Ethan shook the suggestions away. "I'd rather you stayed. I'd feel better knowing you have my back. If you're comfortable with however this plays out," Ethan told him, which wasn't entirely a lie. He did like the idea of having an extra pair of eyes and ears he thought he might be able to trust. But if John was trying to double-cross him, he wanted him close just as much.
"So, what do we do next?" John asked, using his shoulder to push him from the door to the interior of the room.

Ethan walked over to his bed, retrieving the snub-nosed .38 from under the pillow. He extended his arm, handing it to John. John looked at the weapon like it was an unidentified form of the plague, grabbing the grip with his thumb and forefinger, then with his left hand once he realized it was heavier than he expected.

"I don't do guns," John said. "I wouldn't even know how to use this thing."

"Well, hopefully just pull the trigger. If you have to use it then we are already in trouble." Ethan pointed at different parts of the firearm as he spoke. "The pointy piece in the back is the hammer. When you pull the trigger, that goes back and then snaps down firing a bullet. The cylinder will automatically rotate. Rinse and repeat."

"What about a safe button or something? I don't want to accidentally put a bullet in my leg."

Ethan shook his head. "Those don't come with a safety, I don't think." Ethan had never held a gun until a year ago. He wasn't all that brushed up on firearms or what functions they all had himself. "It takes a bit of commitment to get that trigger pulled. It isn't going to just go off."

"What do you think the odds are I'll need it?"

Ethan shrugged. "Hopefully not at all. But I think I might know where we will get our first lead."

"Where?" A curious look came over John's face as he asked the question.

"Beaver once told me about a house on the other side of the ridge. He said there were a lot of rumors that they were selling drugs. Maybe manufacturing. I think we need to go there."

John raised his eyebrow suspiciously, still holding the revolver as though it could bite him at any second. "Why would we need to go there? More importantly, why would you *want* to?"

"If they are in the trade, they might be supplied by Vargas. Or their supplier is. Or they know of him. He could be staying there. There's a lot of reasons we need to go over there."

John raised a finger to reiterate the fact he had a point to make. "Let's assume any one of those is true. They won't be too thrilled with you asking questions, you add more enemies to your list, and it might hasten your time of death."

Ethan shook his head. "I wasn't planning on talking to them. We can get there through the woods; they won't even know we're there. Then, we scope out the house and see how many people are there. If Vargas is there, we have proof. Not to mention we would know which direction he would be coming from. If he isn't there, they don't know we ever came by. We just end up where we are now, which is with nothing."

"What about cameras? What about dogs? We don't know what steps they've taken to make sure people can't do what you're planning to do." John finally lowered his arm, growing slightly more comfortable with the fact he had a gun in his hand. "You can't assume they'd be any less dangerous than the dealers in the city just because there might be fewer eyes on them."

"I'm going either way. You can stay here and make sure no one shows up, but you'd be dealing with them alone."

John shook his head, gingerly sliding the pistol into his pocket. "No, I should go. Make sure you don't get yourself killed. I would like to put it on record that it is a terrible idea."

"Probably," Ethan said. He grabbed his rifle, rechecking the chamber to make sure a live round was seated. Then he opened the drawer to his dresser to retrieve a set of binoculars, which he pulled over his head, letting them lay flat on his chest.

As the two men exited the cabin, Ethan locked the door. Something he rarely did. Something he loved about being secluded in the woods because he never had to do that until now.

"It'll be about a half-hour walk. Mostly uphill. But once we hit the crest of the ridge, we'll have to slow down so we don't make any noise."

John nodded his understanding.

"Let's go."

Chapter 18

Ethan led John around the left side of his property into the woods, where they followed a dried creek bed two miles to the ridge. Ethan had chosen this path because the parcel of land the woods sat on didn't belong to Beaver. He knew the ravine on the right would be slightly quicker because the woods were not as thick with underbrush, but there was a high likelihood of running into Beaver. Either he would see them headed toward the ridge and then up and over toward the other cabin, or he would stop them to ask what they were doing. Either way, Ethan didn't feel like having that conversation, especially after Beaver had warned him about coming up on those types of people out of the blue.

The two miles, which would have taken less than half an hour under normal conditions, had taken twice as long. Ethan stopped at the base of the ridge. The bare trees did little to conceal them, so he had loaned John a brown jacket and told him to wear black pants.

"We need to be somewhat mindful walking up this hill. They won't be able to see us, but they might hear us. Once we hit the crest, I'll see what we're looking at, then go from there."

"I don't remember you being so fast and loose when you were practicing law," John whispered.

He didn't know a lot about how Ethan practiced. "Just don't make too much noise."

John nodded to confirm he understood the instructions. They crept low up the hill, stopping every twenty feet or so to listen to determine if whoever was on the other side was roaming their portion of the hill.

Once at the crown of the hill, Ethan and John kneeled behind a large fallen tree. Their position overlooked the house, and Ethan noted that a trail wound down to the backside of the house.

He pulled the binoculars from his chest to get a better look. He made some adjustments on the zoom and focus, then found the building. *The cabin* was a loose description Beaver had used to describe it. He supposed it was a cabin by definition, but by appearance, it was a hut. It had been crudely built by someone who just wanted a place to sleep in the woods. It was about the same size as Ethan's, barley. He guessed three or four rooms. The door and window he could see from his position had been repurposed from another structure.

He continued scanning the area, away from the house toward the dirt path that led to it. He stopped at two vehicles. A newer 4x4 black truck with wheels ready to attack the most rugged trails. Parked behind the truck was a black car. Even though Ethan couldn't see the car's emblem from his angle, he knew it looked exactly like the car he had spotted at the motel. The one car he believed Vargas might have chosen to drive.

"I think Vargas might be here," Ethan said quietly.

John looked at him doubtfully.

"I want you to stay here," he said, removing the binoculars from his neck and handing them to John. If anything happens, I want you to go down the way we came. If you go straight, you'll eventually hit the road, which will lead to my cabin." He pointed to add to the instruction: "If you get to the road, the cell service is better. If you get to the cabin, just go."

"I'm not going to leave until I know you're safe."

Ethan shook his head. "If they spot me and they're selling or making drugs out of there, they won't just let me walk away. There's nothing you'll be able to do."

"Then don't do anything stupid," John commanded.

"I'll do my best," Ethan told him. Then, he continued down the trail toward the back of the hut. Halfway between the fallen log at the top of the ridge and the hut, two men came out. Ethan stopped, pressing himself against a tree. The two men lit cigarettes, talking, and pointing in various directions.

The short wide one in the tattered overalls reminded Ethan of a *Beverly Hillbillies* character before moving into the high life. Ethan figured if it came down to it, he could beat the man in a fight. Though, he suspected the man had found that to be the case many times before, learning it was better to shoot first and ask questions later. He might be able to outrun the man, but he couldn't outrun his bullets.

The man beside the hillbilly was tall, athletic looking. The muscle in their group of how-ever-many. His jeans fit, unlike the overalls on the other man. He also wore a shirt that had, at one point, probably been white. The man would rub his hands on his shirt, almost compulsively, which Ethan guessed, was how it had become so stained since he acquired it.

The two men turned their focus to the truck. Once they started walking toward it, Ethan continued his descent, cutting off from the main trail to a game trail that offered more cover from the undergrowth and young saplings. He followed the path to the back of the house, where he sat only twenty-five yards from a back window.

He didn't have the best view. The window was slightly elevated to his position and just as dirty as the taller man's shirt. Ethan wondered if he had even tried to clean the window with the garment.

Ethan rose himself to his knees, allowing for a better view, but also most exposure. He could see movement inside the room, but little else. He looked back to the ridge's peak, but John was hidden behind all the brush, which made him feel better. Ethen then looked for the trail but once the trees swallowed the entry point, he couldn't see it, also bringing him some comfort.

When he returned his attention to the window, he saw a new face appear, scanning the outside.

Ethan lowered himself slightly to his knees, thankful the man didn't seem to notice. His thick beard made him look like a bear. It wasn't Vargas.

Ethan knew that meant at least three people were commonly in the shack. One or two possibly lived there and guarded whatever was inside. He knew his cabin had felt more crammed with just adding John. He couldn't imagine the tightness three grown men would produce. Of course, as he noticed unpatched holes in the roof and parts of the side, he wondered if it was possible none of them lived there at all. It could just as easily have been where they produced and distributed their drugs, moonshine, or whatever they had inside.

The man left the window and disappeared behind a wall. Ethan sat there a few more moments before deciding to leave. Before he turned to crawl back into the thicker part of the woods, another face appeared, doing their own examination of the area. Ethan recognized the face right away from the stern eyes and the white beard with yellow stains. Beaver turned from the window. Ethan felt a surge of betrayal. It was a familiar and uncomfortable feeling he pushed aside, letting anger replace it.

※

Ethan found John still kneeling behind the log. His eyes were in the binoculars. Not wanting to startle him, which could cause John to react, betraying their position, Ethan ruffled some leaves near him. John dropped the binoculars, turning toward Ethan. Ethan crept closer, then dropped to sit behind the log.

"Did you see anything?"

"Took some big bags to the truck. The two guys who came out went back in. Nothing since."

"We need to get back to the cabin."

John followed Ethan back, neither one saying a word. Ethan spent the entire walk back, running what he had seen through his mind. He tried to make excuses that would make sense for Beaver to be in the hut. He tried to convince himself Beaver went to tell them to shut it all down, that he didn't want that shit going on in his backyard. But with the look in his eyes as he scanned the exterior, Ethan knew there had been another reason he had been inside the cabin. He was either part of the operation or he was a buyer.

Ethan reeled his mind in. No matter what Beaver's involvement, it didn't mean he knew about Vargas. It didn't mean he knew about Ethan or his history. It didn't even mean Beaver was involved with those men. He knew Beaver took care of his neighbors—the man took time out of his life to teach Ethan the basics of living off the land. Ethan abandoned the thoughts when his head started to hurt, going up to the cabin instead of letting his mind roam any longer.

Once inside, Ethan locked the door behind him. He grabbed two new logs, placing them in the stove before tossing in a match. He stood there with his hands hovering over the slightly warm steel, desperate to warm them. Ethan didn't feel cold, but his hands were shaking. He didn't want to admit it was his anger growing.

"What did you see?" John finally asked, sitting at the kitchen table, pouring them each a shot of whiskey.

"What makes you think I saw anything?"

John gave him a look. "You were quiet the whole walk back. You looked like you were about to punch every tree you passed. I've seen that look before. I know what it means."

Ethan shook his head, joining John at the table. "It just means Beaver might not be who I thought he was."

"Was he there?" John may have tried to cover up his surprise, but it didn't work.

"He was inside."

"What are you going to do with that information?" John twirled his drink in his hands, watching the dark liquid twirl in the glass.

"You should call that investigator you used to work with. Mason Sharp? See what he can pull up on him."

John's eyes narrowed questioningly. "You want me to ask him to run a check on a guy named Beaver? Do you have a little more to go on? Date of birth, real name? You know, stuff he can actually look into."

Ethan sighed, knowing he didn't. "No. I think I know how we can get it, though."

"How do you suppose you'll go about doing that?"

"I can get in and out of his cabin in a matter of minutes. We should have plenty of time to find something inside to tell us his real name."

John shook his head adamantly. "Even if you can, that doesn't mean you should. You already have someone out here messing with you. You need friends, not enemies."

"How do I know he isn't working with my enemy? I can't trust him if I don't know why he was out there."

"I wish I'd never come here," John said. His voice portrayed it as a joke, but Ethan knew there was a great deal of truth in there, too.

"It isn't too late for you to go back home."

John nodded, "Yes, it is."

Chapter 19

Ethan and John crossed the woods to the right of Beaver's cabin. They entered the cluttered yard and stood there a moment. Ethan assumed that if Beaver had already returned, he would see them. He would approach them, and then Ethan could simply pretend he needed the old man's advice on making jerky or a blanket. After several long seconds, no one came.

Ethan told John to find something significant to conceal himself near where they stood. "If he comes through the woods from their hut, you'll spot him first. If he drives up the driveway, you'll spot him. Whistle like a bird if you do."

"Where will you be?" John's question floated for a moment as he provided his own answer. "You're not really going to go inside, are you?"

"We need a name. You said it yourself."

"Of all the possible ways to go about finding out someone's name, you choose to sneak into his house and look through his belongings?"

Ethan handed John his rifle. "Scoot back to that tree. If I have to leave or he catches me on his property, I don't want him to know I have a lookout. I'd rather him think it was just me."

"What difference does it make?"

Ethan shrugged. "Probably none. But it would undoubtedly make him pretty suspicious."

"Make it quick. He could be right around the corner, for all you know."

Ethan turned, making his way to Beaver's homestead. The cabin would be easy enough to get into since the back half was covered in tarps, only good enough to keep out the snow and rain but little else. Ethan wondered how many wild animals had gotten into the cabin since his remodel had begun sometime before Ethan moved in down the way. He lifted back the green tarp far enough to slip between it and the wood frame.

The room he found himself in wasn't a room at all. It was Beaver's version of an attached garage. Hunting, fishing, tools, and small farming instruments were organized in various sections of the area. Nearest the door, fifteen feet away, was a massive pile of wood, which reminded Ethan how far behind he was on his own stack. No matter how today played out, he needed to ensure he wouldn't freeze over winter, or confronting Vargas would mean very little.

Ethan went to the door, testing the knob to make sure it turned and was pleased to find it did. He went into the rest of the structure, which had more order than Ethan would have guessed. On the outside, Beaver was organized chaos, from his appearance to the mounds of trash strewn across his lot. However, inside, he had order. Everything seemed to have a place where it belonged. Ethan doubted any of them ventured far away.

He turned in the room slowly to allow himself to take it all in. The cabin was dark, even for midday. Ethan noticed several gas lamps scattered along the walls, hanging with charred ropes exposed. There was also a wood-burning stove, slightly larger than Ethan's. There was a long, upholstered couch in the center of the living area, a couple of small tables, and a bookcase on either side of the room, each past capacity. The blinds in the windows were open, allowing the sun full access to the room.

From where he stood, John's head just barely revealed itself, mostly tucked behind a tree. The kitchen was like Ethan's, except Beaver had some sort of ice box rather than a refrigerator. Ethan noticed then that the cabin had no electricity. No television. Part of Ethan was envious of this. He knew it was a form of freedom he wasn't ready for. Before the bookcase, a staircase was to the left of the living area. From where he stood, Ethan could tell it was a loft, likely where Beaver slept. Ethan made another turn, trying to decide where the man would keep important things. No matter how off-grid he was, he had taxes, a birth certificate, or old letters or diaries. Regardless, there had to be *something* inside there that would tell Ethan the man's real name.

He started with the bookcases. The one to the left had a series of drawers under the stacks of books, the other only held books. He worked through them systematically from left to right. The drawers mostly held other, smaller books and random decks of cards held together by rubber bands, but nothing that looked like an official document. In the last drawer, he saw a black box—the only thing in the drawer.

He picked up the box, flipping it over for closer examination. The top of the box had a plexiglass covering revealing a Purple Heart atop a Bronze Star. A small pendant had been pressed into the tan velvet below the medals that read *Sargent Carson*. Ethan felt little joy in the discovery. He had no way of knowing if Carson was his name, a friend's name, or someone else in his family. They could've been awards he received or awards someone had left to him. He certainly had made no effort to display them.

Ethan put the item back in the drawer and closed it. He turned to check on John. Ethan didn't have time to look for him before he saw Beaver coming out of the wood line toward the back of his property. Ethan froze in the living room, his whole body weighed down by invisible lead chains. It looked like Beaver was heading for the same entry point he had taken. When Beaver reached the halfway point between the woods and the house, Ethan broke free of the chains, hastily heading for the front door.

☯

Ethan stopped on the porch when he heard the heavy footfalls of Beaver just inside the cabin. He stopped somewhere in the middle of the building and then started moving again. Ethan knew he couldn't make a move. If he went to either side of the building, he would be easy to spot. If he went down the narrow drive, he would either be spotted or heard. He looked over to where John had been but could only see the dead underbrush.

Ethan decided to be proactive, turning back toward the door. When he did, he saw John peek his head over the brush. His eyes were narrow as if asking what Ethan thought he was doing. Ethan knocked.

The heavy footsteps grew closer, and without pause, the door opened. Beaver stood across the threshold, a cup of coffee in his left hand. He seemed welcoming, but Ethan couldn't help but think of him at the hut. The unpleasant familiarity of betrayal rushed through him again. He grit his teeth and steeled himself, offering a smile to Beaver.

"Ethan," Beaver's voice was gravely as he spoke. "I didn't expect you comin' by."

"I came by a few days ago, and you weren't here. Just thought I'd try again."

Beaver nodded as he accepted what he was being told. "Come on in. Would you like some coffee?"

"No, thank you," Ethan said. "Too late in the day for me. I'd be up all night."

"Suit yourself. What brings you by?" Beaver stopped at his counter in the kitchen, leaning his back against it for support. He wrapped both hands around his mug to warm them. Ethan noticed the woodstove had been started as well.

Ethan realized he hadn't thought of an excuse for his presence. Then he recalled the ones he had given John. "I got that deer the other day. I was wondering if you had any suggestions for making jerky out of it."

Beaver shrugged. "You have an oven, right?" Ethan nodded.

"Season it. Cook it at two hundred until it's leathery. Ain't too hard."

Ethan grinned, raising his hands to his side, showing how silly he felt for making the trip for such a simple question. "I appreciate it. Guess I'll get going and leave you to yourself." Ethan turned to walk away when Beaver stopped him.

"Why don't you tell me why you really stopped by?"

Ethan turned to face Beaver. His eyes passed the window but he didn't see John. Frozen hands twisted at his stomach, "What do you mean?"

"I mean you didn't walk out here just to ask about jerky."

"I guess I just wanted some human interaction," he lied. "It's a bit different out here than in the city."

Beaver nodded his agreeance. "Why now?"

"What do you mean?"

"You've been out here a year, boy. You ain't never come by just 'cause you was feelin' a little lonely."

"Can I ask you something?" Ethan felt his heart begin to thud. The beating sound was so heavy in his ears, that he feared Beaver would hear it too.

"You can ask whatever you want. Doesn't mean I'll answer it."

"What's your real name?" Ethan let his legs widen a little. He didn't think Beaver would attack him for such a simple question, but then, he didn't really know the man at all.

Beaver studied him for a moment. The silence grew uncomfortable to the point Ethan tried to take the question back. "Sorry, I was just curious. I'll go now."

"It really ain't none of your business. Don't know why you're so curious, but if you must know, my God-given name was Michael Carson."

"Was?"

"It ain't no more. Now, it's Beaver."

"I don't intend to pry. Why give up your whole life? Even your name?"

A smirk spread across Beaver's face, visible even beneath his thick beard. "Is that something you're willin' to answer, too?"

Ethan tried to conceal his discomfort. He knew he failed.

"I didn't think so," Beaver said, turning and setting his mug down on the counter. "A man can bury parts of himself for a lot of reasons. Sometimes, for the people he loves; to protect them. Sometimes for himself; because they scare even him. But if he doesn't do it for one or the other, he'll lose himself." Beaver leaned back further on the counter before recoiling back with a deep exhale. "I guess you could say, I lost myself. So, I decided to be someone else."

"I get that," Ethan said.

"I thought you might."

Chapter 20

Ethan returned to the cabin alone. He had no good way of signaling to John or collecting him from his hidden position behind Beaver's. Ethan hoped his friend had taken the opportunity to leave when Beaver was distracted by Ethan and their conversation. However, when Ethan arrived back home to find it empty, he worried John may have gotten turned around in the woods. It wasn't hard to do. If he entered a thicket or even found all the trees to start looking the same—which happened often out there—he could easily find himself walking in circles.

Ethan stood on his front porch, letting the afternoon sun blast his face, providing a nice contrast to the cool wind brushing his flesh from the east. He decided it was too risky to go into the woods looking for John. He needed to stay there so John wouldn't find himself worried Ethan had gotten lost. However, he also knew he couldn't go yelling for his friend, which would set off alarms for Beaver, especially since Ethan hadn't mentioned having any guests in their two encounters.

Instead, Ethan went down to the wood pile, retrieving his axe from under the overhang on his way. He lifted a large log onto the chopping log, bringing a solid swing down. This task was multifaceted for him. For one, it would fill the need for more wood as winter approached. Secondly, it would give an unmistakable sound for John to follow if he were out in the woods wandering around. And third, it would allow Ethan's mind to stop chasing uncertainties. The racing thoughts of where John was at that moment, what it was Beaver had run from—his own demons he had decided to leave as well—and his intrusive thoughts on what Beaver was doing at the hillbillies' hut. It had been Beaver who'd warned him of the place. Of course, people often tried to prevent others from knowing their dark deeds.

Ethan had seen it hundreds of times. Criminals ratted on their accomplices, painting themselves as innocent bystanders or, in some cases, pulling a sleight of hand with the skill of a magician to distract the authorities so they could get away with whatever they were doing. If Beaver had kept Ethan away from the hut, Ethan would not have known what was going on, nor would he have known about Beaver's involvement. If heat came down on them, he would be in the shadows. Only having the word of the hillbillies over his own.

At that moment, Ethan decided he needed to act. He needed to know the depth of their operation. If they were a small-time setup, they may not have any connection to Vargas. But if they were moving a lot of product, Vargas could have them in his pocket. If that were the case, Beaver could've been the one to betray his whereabouts. The one person out there he thought he could trust could be the very person who fed him to the wolves.

Ethan's swings picked up in intensity as the concept built in his mind. He swung the axe harder, moving through the logs without recognition. He had come through the ashes once. He could do it again, he decided. He was tired of running. He was tired of hiding. If they wanted to kill him, they would have to burn with him.

As the thoughts got his blood to a near boil, he heard John call out to him, bringing him back down to a stable level almost instantly. The pressure he hadn't felt building in his chest, shoulders, and neck all released at once. His breathing was heavy from the rapid chopping, and despite the cold breeze, he felt sweat spilling from his brow. He turned to face John, putting the axe head in the dirt using the handle as support.

"Where were you?" Ethan asked through labored breaths.

John looked around bewildered. "I don't know. I saw you talking to the old man, so I took the opportunity to back out. I ended up walking in circles out there." John gingerly pulled the revolver from his pocket, laying it on a log. "I heard the chopping and followed that. Which, I might add, isn't as easy as you'd think when all the sounds echo off everything."

"I'm glad you're okay," Ethan said, patting John on the shoulder. "I was going to come up with a plan B if you didn't arrive soon."

John pointed to the pile of chopped logs, easily a week's worth of wood. "It looks like you were going hard on those logs."

Ethan looked down at his work. He had been chopping on auto-pilot, paying no attention to the process. Simply swinging, lifting logs, and swinging again. "I got a name for you. Think that'll be enough for Mason Sharp?"

"It's a good start. What is it?"

"Michael Carson."

"I'll go inside and make the call to Sharp. Great investigator," John turned to head into the cabin when Ethan stopped him.

"Do you mind going into town?"

John stopped and faced him with doubt in his eyes. "Why?"

"Better service for one. Also, I wasn't planning on two people being here for a prolonged time. I don't have the supplies to get us through much longer and then myself after you leave. I'll pay you back, of course."

"What am I supposed to get?"

"I'll get you a list."

Ethan led John inside and scribbled down a list of things he really would need but weren't necessities—at least not for a few more weeks. He added eggs, bacon, coffee, gasoline, bottled water, flour, and cooking oil. Then, he added a couple of items that would require John to go to a second store to buy more time. For that list, he added a chainsaw chain, 2-stroke oil, and chains for his tires.

John's hesitancy was apparent throughout the process. He never questioned it, though. Ethan handed John the sheet of paper. "I need to go scout the river to see if there's any trout in there. If I'm not here when you are, I'll put a key under the axe head."

John's head cocked in disappointment. "Don't do anything stupid."

"I'm just checking the river. We're going to need the food."

"I can go with you to do that, then go to town."

"No," Ethan said, more frustrated than he had intended. "I don't want them to close before you get there. Plus, I want to see if the P.I. can uncover any more information on Beaver." Even knowing his real name, Ethan knew he would only call him by his chosen one.

John nodded doubtfully as he stuffed the list into his pocket. "I'll be back as soon as I can."

"I'll probably be here. If not, start a fire, and feel free to cook something from the fridge."

John left the cabin, looking back toward Ethan once before getting into his car. Once it started and backed up, Ethan grabbed his rifle. He checked the chamber before he grabbed the keys to his truck. He had just bought himself a couple of hours. He was going to watch the hillbillies. One way or another, he would end the night with more answers than he had then.

Chapter 21

Ethan stepped out to the front porch, locking the door behind him. The sun was already halfway tucked behind the treetops. Rays of orange blasted from behind them. As the sun set, it took with it the warmth it had provided through most of the day. The eastern wind had picked up intensity, biting Ethan's face as soon as he exposed it to the world. He pulled his hood up to block some of the wind before running to his truck.

He sat his rifle barrel down in the passenger seat. Ethan twisted the keys, hoping the truck wouldn't give him any resistance. The warmer day should have made it easier for the truck to start, as the fluid would be able to flow with more ease. He smiled broadly, almost cartoonishly, when the vehicle roared to life. He backed away, watching his cabin from the rearview as he drove down his drive.

Ethan went right out of his driveway and continued for a mile before reaching State Road 38. He took another right onto the main road, following it for two miles. He pulled into a small opening separating the woods from the road. He adjusted his truck to be backed into it. The spot was used by hunters who didn't have private property. About seventy square acres of the woods behind and in front of him was public land, open to anyone. So it wouldn't be weird for him to be parked there if someone were to pass by. His property butted up to the land. He realized anyone who knew that could easily access his plot of land by coming through this section. No one would question a vehicle parked there, and unless they kept the vehicle there for a few days straight, it wouldn't raise any suspicion.

He looked to the right where anyone leaving the hut would have to come from. The road was a dead end just past the hut. Ethan suspected they could use ATVs or small four-wheelers to cut through the woods. But the woods could be hazardous to travel in the light of day. As the sun continued to set, leaving him in near darkness, he knew the woods would be almost impossible to traverse. They would have to use lights. If the roars of their motors didn't set off any wariness, the lights certainly would.

No, he decided, they would take the road. He could follow them from either direction.

Then, almost like fate, he saw beams of light bouncing from the gravel road he was watching. He lowered his head, watching from his peripheral as the black pickup he saw parked in the driveway earlier pulled onto the main road. They turned left toward him. He kept his eyes low, noticing they had stopped right in front of him.

His head followed his eyes when they raised to meet the cold stare of the short bald hillbilly. The man's lower lip was fat where his tongue pressed against the back, his jaws moved side-to-side chewing on his tongue.

Ethan rolled his window down, grabbing the stock of his rifle with his opposite hand.

"Everything okay over there?" The man asked.

Ethan stuck his head out of the window, shouting over the grumbles of his engine. "Yeah, I was just about to head home."

"You hunting out there?" The taller man behind the driver eyed Ethan with cold, empty eyes.

"Tried. No luck today."

"Yeah, most of the deer this time of year hunker down over there," he said, pointing to the opposite side of the road with his thumb. Ethan knew that wasn't true. Just a few days ago, he tagged a buck from this side on his property. He figured the man said this to anyone he saw parked there, wanting to keep as many people from accidentally stumbling across their hut as possible.

"I'll keep that in mind. I'm James, by the way," he blurted the name out so quickly he surprised himself. It was only a partial lie, though. James was his middle name.

"Nice to meet ya. I'm Mark, but most people call me Trapper." He pointed to the tall man beside him. "This here is Gus."

Ethan offered a smile. "Pleasure to meet you both. I'll see you around."

"Count on it," Mark told him. "Remember, stick to that side of the road, and you'll be fine." The short man gave Ethan a wink before driving off.

Ethan waited a few seconds, then pulled out behind them.

Ethan had done one stakeout with a P.I. when he worked at the DA office. It ended with them trailing a subject. While it had been over a decade, and he wasn't taking notes, he remembered the basics. Keep a precise distance, slow down every so often to let them gain separation, and if they park, keep moving to park somewhere else. The downside now was that his truck was loud and not ambiguous.

Ethan followed Mark and Gus to the Hillside Motel. They pulled in, finding a spot in front of the long row of doors. Ethan pulled into a business across the street he didn't bother to get the name of. He found a large cement truck parked horizontally to the motel. He pulled in behind the truck so he could see the motel, turning the truck off to kill the lights and rumble of the engine. It was a risk since he would have to rely on the thing starting again if they were going to make a second run.

Mark got out of the truck first. The short man had to jump from his seat down to the pavement below. He shouted something at Gus before waving his arms around at the motel. Gus got out shortly after, gripping a large black duffle bag tightly in his giant paws.

The two men walked to their left to a room with a white jalopy car parked outside, which looked like it struggled to run more than Ethan's truck. He didn't know exactly what was in the bag, but he wondered how anyone driving a car like that could afford a duffle bag of anything worth much. Of course, a car like that didn't draw as much attention parked outside the Hillside Motel as even the truck.

Ethan set a timer on his phone. He would wait ten minutes before leaving because any longer than that, he risked someone spotting him. Besides, he reasoned, if they were there more than ten minutes, they may be planning to stay the whole night.

After Mark knocked on the motel room door, it was opened almost immediately by a shirtless man standing right in the middle of Mark and Gus's height. His hair had been pulled back into a lazy ponytail. The man looked frail, with bones visible through his flesh. He was like a skeleton with a thin blanket thrown over it out of courtesy.

All three men vanished behind the door.

⁂

Exactly eight and a half minutes later, Mark and Gus exited the room, wasting no time to get to the truck. They fired it up, squealing their tires as they backed away from their parking spot. They sped to the exit of the motel parking lot, then slowed as

Mark pulled out and turned left, continuing in the opposite direction of their hut.

Ethan waited a few seconds until their taillights were just barely visible in the darkness before willing his truck to start, which did on the second attempt. He turned right out of the lot, pressing hard on the gas to catch up. Once he could see their lights, he let up.

Ethan had been so focused on his distance, he hadn't paid any attention to what direction they were driving or what roads they had taken. He had made two left turns and a right while following the truck. Ethan thought about starting his navigation app to see where they were, but the truck turned again before he could consider it further. This time, they were in a residential neighborhood.

It was one of the few in the area. Ethan recognized this one as Woodland Pines, an ambitious plan during its conception in the '80s. Three decades ago, the neighborhood was supposed to sit on an entire 18-hole golf course with French-style homes made of light stone and steep rooftops. Unfortunately for the developers, they were too far ahead of their time. Nothing else came after their development went up, meaning they had to start selling houses at a loss just to get out from under the project. The golf course was never constructed, and now the neighborhood was just an out-of-place three-mile square surrounded by corn and bean fields. There had been rumors of a strip mall coming in the next couple of years in the field across from the neighborhood, but that too may have been too hefty of a goal to strive for.

The truck pulled into the driveway of a two-story home. The true beauty of the French-inspired architecture was hidden behind layers of green mildew and browned bricks. The steep roof was stained with dark patches from more moisture. The large windows had been covered from the inside with what looked like cheap blinds.

Ethan continued driving to the next block, where the road turned right. He made a three-point turn, killing his lights when he had fully turned around so he could see the house.

Like at the motel, Mark and Gus got out of the truck with a duffle bag, knocked on the door, and spent eight minutes inside. When they left, Ethan stayed where he was. He could follow them all night, but that wouldn't tell him anything more than what he had already learned. Which was that they were making deliveries in duffle bags. Either money, drugs, or both. Perhaps it was something else, like firearms, but it was all speculation unless he did something to find out more. If he did nothing, he would only be assuming they were delivering drugs for Vargas.

He ran his cold hand over his rough beard, forcing out a heavy breath. He knew he had to go inside. Ethan focused his attention on each of the houses surrounding the one where Mark and Gus had stopped. All looked weathered, but most were more cared for than that one. Some had cars parked in the driveway, but most didn't. A few houses had lights on inside, but he guessed he could get in and out quickly if he parked facing the neighborhood exit.

Ethan knew he would have at least fifteen minutes to get out of the neighborhood before the police arrived. Assuming a neighbor called for some reason. He knew whoever was inside that house wouldn't be making the call.

He put his truck in gear, pulling away from the curb toward the house. He parked directly in front of it. Ethan retrieved one of his hunting masks from the glove compartment. He pulled it over his face, removed his wedding ring from his hand, and placed it into the cup holder. He got out; his rifle tucked close to his body in hopes of concealing it from anyone who might be watching from the windows. He didn't give his mind time to think about his decision because he knew he'd talk himself out of going inside.

Chapter 22

Ethan went directly to the front door, knocking twice. He kept himself just off the center of the door. From the other side, he heard a male's voice saying something about forgetting. Blood thundered in his ears, causing his head to start hurting. His stomach twisted when the footsteps reached the door; for a moment, he thought he might get sick. A rapid flash of heat purged his body as soon as the door opened. Ethan threw his body into the half-open door, knocking the opener to the ground with a rattling thud. His breath exploded from his chest.

Ethan saw another man sitting on a couch in the room adjacent to the door. He fumbled for something on the glass table in front of him. Ethan guessed a gun. He raised the rifle, the barrel in line with the man's face.

"Don't," was all Ethan said. Then he looked down at the man on the floor. "Go sit with him."

Ethan followed closely, then grabbed the gun from the table when the man he knocked down sat. He slid it into the front of his jeans, careful not to leave prints the best he could. He wished he had worn gloves.

The glass table was covered with plastic-wrapped bricks of a white substance. Smaller bags and scales were scattered on the table.

For the first time, he looked at the men. He felt his stomach tighten again when he realized they were not men at all. They were no older than nineteen or twenty. If not for the clear signs of cutting dope to sell, they would be typical college-looking kids. The one he had knocked down with the door had curly red hair that began to spill over his face. The other one wore thick-rimmed glasses that bugged his eyes out, magnifying them to at least twice their natural size.

Both wore cheap polo shirts and dark sweatpants. The ginger-haired boy wore flip-flops—one missing, likely lost in Ethan's entry—and the other wore house slippers. He could see them shaking, their eyes pleading for him to spare their lives. These were not hard-nosed criminals—just dumb kids.

"I'm not going to hurt you," Ethan promised. He lowered his voice a whole octave to further distort his identity. Not that either of them would have been able to identify him anyway. "Where'd you get the stash?"

The one in glasses spoke, "From a couple of rednecks. We buy from them to sell at school. Tuition is crazy expensive. Take it, man! You can have it!"

"I don't want the drugs," Ethan said as he lowered the rifle from his face, keeping the barrel in their direction. He had pointed it at the sofa between them, though he doubted they would know the difference. "I want to know who their supplier is."

The red-haired boy spoke this time, "We don't know all that. We just tell them when we need more, and they bring it by."

"Do you know Angel Vargas?"

"Who?" They asked in unison. Their hands were shaking.

"Who else do they distribute to?"

"Most everyone, man. They sell everything from bud to ice and guns."

"What about an older man with a white beard? Has he ever come to make deliveries?"

The redhead stammered, "No. Always the same two dudes."

"You two need to focus on school and put this foolishness behind you. Let this be a lesson to you," Ethan scolded as he raised his rifle, bringing it down on the glass top of the table. Everything crashed to the ground. One of the packages tore at the seam, sending a dusting into the air.

"Do you know where they meet their supplier?"

The two shook their heads, on the verge of tears.

Ethan didn't say anything else. He just left. Once outside, He pulled the pistol from his jeans, wiping the grip with the bottom of his shirt before tossing it into the bushes in front of the house. He tucked his rifle close to him again, entering his truck from the passenger side. He had left it running out of fear it wouldn't start if he had to make a quick getaway.

Ethan threw the gear in place, stomping on the gas leaving a small cloud of smoke behind him and his screaming tires.

When he reached home, he shut off the truck, letting his heart rate slow as much as he could. John had already returned. He wondered how long he had been back, but more importantly, how many questions John would have and how he would answer them.

Ethan got out of the truck and was instantly struck by an overwhelming smell of burning wood. It hit him like a train, which seemed odd with the wind blowing from the west. It should've blown the smoke parallel to him, dampening the scent. The smoke from the chimney looked appropriate, but he supposed John could've still overfilled the wood stove.

Ethan pulled his key from his pocket as he ascended the steps, unlocking the door and going inside with one fluid motion. He set the rifle to the side of the door as usual. John was on the sofa, scrolling through channels.

"How was the river?"

"Not bad. Think tomorrow we might be able to stock up on some trout." Ethan crossed the room, finding a spot next to John.

"Do you always stay down there until after ten?"

Ethan pulled his phone from his pocket to double-check the time. It seemed wrong. He had started following Mark and Gus just after 6:30 p.m.

and assumed the whole ordeal had taken less than three hours. "No," Ethan said.

John seemed to pick up on the hesitancy in his voice. "What took so long this time?"

Ethan didn't have the energy to lie. "I followed those hillbillies."

"You what?" John's voice came out coated with anger. "That's a stupid thing to do."

Ethan nodded, realizing then that it probably was one of the worst ideas he had in a while. "I was just tired of not knowing anything. Especially when someone is out there knowing everything about me. I'm tired of being a fucking target."

"You should've let me tag along. What if they saw you following them?"

Ethan's shoulders shot up, "If I took you, I knew you'd try to talk me out of everything."

"Which is exactly what you need," John said, punching Ethan's shoulder.

Ethan told him about the two stops. Then, against his better judgment, about the two college kids he interrogated.

"Wow," John stammered. "That's insane. Did you do anything else?"

"No," Ethan told him honestly.

"Are you sure?"

"Nothing else I could do," Ethan told him. "Mark and Gus were long gone by then. No way to follow them anymore. I had nothing else I could do but come back here."

"Good. I say you let it go. Stick to the original plan."

"Which was what, exactly?" Ethan asked, frustrated.

"Strong defense. You're too far behind the eight ball to play offense now."

"A good defense is a good offense."

John shook his head. "You know your property better than anyone else. You don't know who they sent or how many. If you go digging into other people's lives, especially people you don't know are connected, you're making it that much easier for them. You need to keep in the shadows and wait."

"Might be too late for all that."

"Why?" John asked. "Do you think those kids will tell those two idiots what happened?"

Ethan nodded. "Pretty certain about it." Ethan's chest suddenly stung with a sharp pain as ice replaced his blood. It was as if his heart struggled to pump.

John's eyes became concerned as he reached for Ethan. Ethan pushed his hands away. "Shit," Ethan groaned.

"What?" The concern in John's voice matched the fear in his eyes.

"Mark and Gus stopped to talk to me when they left because they saw me parked in the pull-off near their driveway. If those two kids saw my truck and described it to them, they'll already have a big head start."

"You need to hide the damn thing."

Chapter 23

The next morning, Ethan to the sun kissing his face. He made his morning coffee, leaving a cup on the table for John, before heading back into his room. He sipped from his mug, attempting to suppress the headache that had formed in the back of his head. He twisted his neck from side to side, hoping the tension would release itself, but to no avail. He sat his mug down on his dresser before going into the closet.

He intentionally kept his eyes up, away from the box on the floor. He didn't have the energy to let himself go there. Not this morning. Instead, he scanned the top of the racks until he found what he was looking for. Ethan retrieved a rectangular box, brought it down, and set it on his bed. He flipped the top to reveal a pair of waders. Ethan only wore them in the winter and early spring, so he didn't mind slipping into the inherited pair the previous owners left behind. They weren't too expensive, and he wanted to order his own, but these fit well and had no leaks.

He slipped his legs inside, rearranging the attached boot so his foot could fit comfortably. Then, he repeated the process with his other leg before sliding the shoulder straps on. Then he cursed, realizing he needed to go to the restroom.

After finally getting back into his waders, he grabbed his now-cold coffee before returning to the living room. He nudged John on the shoulder, tossing an old pair of jeans and water-resistant boots down next to him.

"Oh," John said through his remnants of sleep, "I have to go fishing, too?"

"If you want to eat dinner tonight, yes."

"Don't you miss just being able to order a pizza or Chinese takeout?"

Ethan downed the rest of his coffee, which had lost its taste. "Once you eat fresh trout, you'll realize what you've been missing out on."

"How about I stay guard here, you go fishing, and I'll just reap the benefit of your hard work?"

"Get up," Ethan told him. "I made you coffee."

"At least I get that," John said, sitting up. He grabbed his cup, taking a test sip to gauge the temperature. Then he chugged it, catching heat at the end. His face contorted in the discomfort but seemed pleased all the same.

"I'll get the rods. Meet me outside in five minutes."

John groaned something as he stood up to get ready.

Five minutes later, John met Ethan on the porch. "Where is the river?"

Ethan pointed to the opposite side of the house, back toward the ridge. "Runs right between my and Beaver's property into the public land."

"Isn't that where your new friends live?"

Ethan ignored his facetiousness. "No, they are further that way," he said, pointing more to the left.

"Still seems like an unwarranted risk. Can't we just fish on your portion?"

"It's not much. We can start there, but if we want to eat, we have to go where the fish are." Ethan patted the zipped pocket on the front of his waders. "I have protection if we need it."

"That's comforting."

Ethan could hear the river before he saw it. The rushing of water cut through the silence of the woods, even casting a refreshing scent into the air Ethan could never quite describe. The few birds that remained in the late fall sang from the empty branches, greeting Ethan and John to their home with astounding harmony. This was why Ethan never wanted to return to the city.

Most of his life had been spent on the go. Rushing from one place to another, the only slow-down being when he was caught in standstill traffic on I-465 or I-69. There was a spiritual release that happened when the things that towered over him were trees rather than concrete buildings. He no longer felt swallowed by the swarms of people roaming the streets. No more worrying about whether he was going to get a nasty letter about leaving his trashcan on the curb for too long or if a neighbor would become fired up over whether his lawn care crew cut down the neighbor's roses. He had no desire to return to that.

When they reached the bank of the river, John appeared unmoved by the sight. The three-foot depth of crystal-clear water moved gracefully over the rocks and logs below the surface, as unphased by the surroundings as John seemed to be. Ethan handed him a rod with a spinning reel.

"Do you know how to use that?" Ethan asked.

"Yeah, you know my grandpa used to make me go fishing with him as a kid."

"Right," Ethan said, not remembering that at all. "I'll wade down the center and fish the far end of the bank. You can stay on the shore and fish behind me on the near side."

"How many can we keep."

"Five," Ethan told him, "Only one can be brown. But I don't know that they stock many brown trout in here."

"Fine."

Finally, Ethan had to ask, "Don't you find this relaxing?"

"Too quiet," John said before making his first cast upstream.

Ethan walked eight feet into the river, roughly halfway. He made his first cast downstream, losing himself in the quiet.

⚜

Ethan and John had spent the whole morning and most of the early afternoon fishing. The walk back to the cabin had been laced with jokes from Ethan to John about how he had caught all four trout, and John had lost two lures. John mostly ignored the jokes, replying with, "If I had a real fishing pole and not that ancient relic, it would've gone differently." Then he said nothing else.

Ethan took the rods and put them back under the porch. Then he took the four fish, still on the stringer, to the shed. John said he would chop wood so he wouldn't have to watch the carnage.

Ethan wasn't exactly proficient at the task, but better than he was at dressing a deer. He would hardly call it *carnage*. But he was glad to have John chop wood and increase the stack since he only had about half the pile he would need to make it through winter.

Fifteen minutes later, Ethan emerged from the shed with the eight fillets, tossing the leftovers into the woods for the coyotes and raccoons. "Ready for lunch?" Ethan asked, raising the fillets over his head triumphantly.

"Yes! I don't see how you never eat breakfast."

"Because I'm out of eggs, and you didn't grab any last night."

"You have one store in town. It's not my fault they don't stock. A Wal-Mart would spruce this place up," John teased.

"Yeah, right up into the ground."

Ethan unlocked the door, letting John go inside first.

As John stirred the singed logs in the stove to bring life back to the dying fire, Ethan prepped half of the fillets with simple ingredients. He found when food was as fresh as it was there, it was better to highlight the natural flavor than to overpower it. So, he sprinkled some salt, pepper, a few squirts of lemon juice, and a square of butter onto the flesh side. Then he wrapped them in foil, giving them to John to put on the back edges of the woodstove where the heat was at the lowest, so they would cook slowly.

He then turned his focus to wrapping some vegetables he had canned during the late summer, prepared the same way as the fish. In ten minutes, he would prove to John that carry-out was overrated and he was wasting his culinary experiences.

Ethan poured two glasses of Jack Daniels and sat next to John as they waited for lunch to finish cooking.

Once the meal was ready, Ethan unfolded the foiled fish and vegetables between the two of them. Ethan allowed John to take the first bite.

"You weren't kidding!" John's eyes closed, dramatizing the pleasure his tastebuds experienced while eating the fresh fish. "This is the best fish I've ever had. It's not just because I'm hungry, either."

Ethan chuckled, enjoying the sense of calmness he had that day. He didn't know how long it would last, but he wanted to hold onto it as long as possible. "I told you. Can't get anything that fresh back in Indy."

"Sure can't," John agreed.

"What's it like back there, anyway? How is everyone?" Ethan hadn't thought about it until that moment, but he really hadn't engaged John in any conversation about his old home. Of course, there wasn't much there for him to care about. Sure, his parents and John were there. But Kristina's parents blamed him for what happened. His boss thought he was a coward because he ran. And the police did nothing to help ease his mind that they would capture Vargas or whoever he hired to set his home ablaze.

"Why don't you go back and see for yourself?"

"There's no reason I would ever dream of going back there. Besides," he added, "I can't leave the cabin alone now."

"Might be good for you. You might find more answers."

"How do you figure that?"

John leaned back on the sofa, helping the food digest by lengthening his stomach. "You can talk to the people working the case. Maybe they know more. Or by going back, you might remember more."

"Back to what? Last I heard, they built a new house where mine was. The neighbors already spoke to the police. They won't have anything new to tell me."

"Maybe they don't need to," John offered. "I bet just by seeing it with new eyes, you'll remember something. And like I said, talking to one of the lawyers on the case might help shed some light on who's out here harassing you."

"It would take me two or three days for all of that. I have nowhere to stay, and leaving the cabin unguarded that long means I could come back to anything."

"Ask Beaver to watch over the place. And you can crash at my place."

Ethan considered the options. He had thought a few times about reaching out to former colleagues to learn more about Vargas and the case. It might prove more beneficial than not, he decided. "We'll go tomorrow. One day. Then we are back here."

"I think it'll open a lot of closed doors for you." John examined Ethan for a moment, then said, "You'll have to clean yourself up. No one will talk to you looking like that."

"Thanks for the boost of confidence."

"Think you'll get anything in just a day?"

"I can't ask Beaver to watch the place, I'm not even sure I trust him anymore. If I'm going to do it, a day's all I have."

"Fair enough," John looked over to the kitchen. "Say, is there any more of that fish?"

Chapter 24

They left early the next morning, while the cover of darkness still shielded them from the potential of anyone seeing Ethan's truck driving down the road. John had offered repeatedly to drive, but Ethan was concerned if Mark or Gus went looking around, they might find his truck parked behind the empty cabin. He was already on edge enough knowing that Vargas was probably watching as they packed up the truck at 5 a.m. before pulling through the inch of snow that had fallen just after midnight. The tracks would tell someone they left. To counter that, he moved two cameras to angle the house from the front as well as the rear.

The drive back to Indianapolis would take nearly three hours. By then, the world would be moving. Ethan argued they should've left at 3 a.m. so they could make some stops while the world slept. With fewer people being awake, there would be fewer people to see them, which was ideal considering Ethan didn't know how many others Vargas may have helping him.

Ethan took a razor to his face for the first time in weeks, leaving his face uncomfortably smooth. It itched, it made him look too young, but it also made him look like he did a year ago. How people in Indianapolis would recognize him. Ethan even took the trimmers to his head, cutting his hair just short enough to not look straggly. It gave his hair uniformity, but it also hid under his cap without spewing out untamed.

John slept most of the drive, which Ethan didn't mind. He liked the silence. The original plan had been to park on Wabash Street, which sat somewhere in the middle of the Prosecutor's Office and the City/County Building. Ethan wasn't comfortable going into either building. He knew he would waste too much time catching up, explaining to everyone where he had been, why he gave up practicing law, and have to deal with obligatory condolences from people who'd already sent cards as well as those who never got the chance. Instead, he decided to wait on Wabash, where he knew Grant Thompson would pass by on his way to or from court.

Grant was a big-city personality trapped in a mid-size market. He kept his role in the prosecutor's office to keep his conscious clear. Grant's tastes were expensive, and while the public sector paid better in law than it did in other arenas, it wasn't enough to fund his expensive style. He bought Armani and Hugo Boss suits second-hand that were two or three seasons out of date. Grant drove a six-year-old BMW that another lawyer had sold him when they upgraded to a Tesla. He dyed his hair dark, did facial exercises, and started each day with 100 pushups. He looked like the sane version of Christian Bale in *American Psycho*—if he had played a lawyer.

Ethan didn't know Grant's schedule for the day, but he knew most courts took lunch around noon, and the office did the same. He would likely be walking to or from one or the other at that time, which meant Ethan and John would have four hours to kill before trying to catch him making the walk.

Ethan drove right past downtown, going north on I-69 before going east on 465 until he found his exit, which would take him down city roads and backstreets around the far east side of Indianapolis and to the place he had once called home.

The community was gated, something he required given his line of work—a lot of good it did for him—which meant he would either have to scale the gate to gain access to the community or hope the gates were open. Of course, even if they were, his truck would be as obvious as an eclipse. Ethan also knew he wouldn't have to be inside the community to get the answers he was searching for.

His house—which he bought ten years before for under $300 thousand and now likely would cost over $2 million—had been burned to the ground with very few items surviving. When he sold the lot a month later, he heard rumors the HOA petitioned to get construction on a new home started right away. What he hoped to find there had nothing to do with his property. Rather, Ethan wanted to remember the roads. Park where he did when he came upon the chaotic scene so he could try to remember what else he saw. John had argued he could use Google Maps to do the same thing, but Ethan didn't think it would be effective. If he was going to waste a whole day doing this, he was going to do it right.

Then he reached the gates to Darkwater Estates. The gates were open, not uncommon when residents were expecting deliveries or service workers. It was more secure to leave the gates open than to give out the codes to random companies. Even though Darkwater didn't have a gate attendant—or at least didn't a year ago—they did have a private patrol unit made up of retired and off-duty police officers, funded by the HOA. Ethan wasn't concerned about them, though. He had no intention of staying there any longer than he needed to.

Ethan turned left into the gate, taking an immediate left onto Spring Rose, following it to the right bend a half mile down the road. At the bend, he eased around it, and went three houses down, stopping within feet of where he had stopped on the day his life changed forever.

The street ran two miles before hitting a T. Along the two miles were roads branching off to the right every block and a half. From where he sat, he could see the house that stood where his belonged. It was a nearly identical replica of the one that burned. John woke, stretching with an obnoxious squeal when he did.

"Are we here?" He asked.

"We're somewhere."

John surveyed his surroundings just before he found Ethan's house. Or the replica of it. "That's downright weird," he said.

"Shut up," Ethan scolded, trying to force his mind back to that afternoon. Barriers had long since been concreted into his mind, reinforced over the past year, making it hard to remember much of anything. He looked at the house again.

The two-story brownstone micro-mansion—a term coined by the realtor who sold them the house—faced the road with a 200-foot driveway, ending at a three-car garage. A walkway broke free from the driveway leading to the front door. While the main floor was lined with arched windows to allow the most sun, the top floor alternated with dormer windows on the gables and egress windows on the flat face. Only half the upper windows actually fed light into the house, while the other half were just for aesthetics. Unlike his home, the replica had several solar panels strategically placed along the steep gray roof on the front side, which made no sense to him. Due to the trees on the property, the eastern side and rear of the house would get more light.

Across the street from where he parked was Mrs. Flanning's house. She had already apologized to him half a dozen times that she hadn't seen what had happened. She had been in her basement, sweating away her morning cocktail on a stair climber, mourning the transition of her twenty-year-old figure into that of a sixty-year-old. The other neighbors had been just as useless.

He took himself back. The streets were flooded with firetrucks, their lights spinning, their sirens screaming, as firemen rushed in all directions with what Ethan could only describe as coordinated anarchy. The police had set up barricades, pushing the rubberneckers back. Ethan finally came to, bursting from his car before he sprinted around the front of his car, rushing down the sidewalk.

A police officer spotted him tossing a sidewalk barricade to the side, continuing his sprint toward his burning home. The officer struck him with the force of a brick wall, taking Ethan straight to the ground forcing every bit of oxygen from his lungs. He reached his hand out; tears began to burn his eyes, making it that much harder to catch his breath.

The officer forced him to his feet and Ethan began screaming for his family.

"Do you live here?" The officer finally clarified.

"Yes! Where's my family? Where's my wife?!"

"We don't know if anyone was inside right now. The fire department said it's a nasty fire, they haven't been able to get inside yet. They are trying to contain it so they can try to get in there."

The calmness in the officer's voice enraged Ethan, he wanted to punch him in the face. How could he be so calm when Ethan didn't even know if his wife was safe? He asked Mrs. Flanning to call his daughter's school when he realized she had followed him during his break toward the house. Then Ethan remembered Kristina had kept Mary out that day. But her car wasn't there.

Ethan looked down the street, the sea of faces all blurring together behind the rapid movement of lights, men in brown and yellow fire suits, and water hoses. Down the road, away from everything else, was a black car. It pulled away from the curb, turning away from the blockade before turning down a street a few blocks away..

Ethan dropped to his knees.

❦

"There was a car," Ethan said. He hadn't noticed the hurt building in his throat until he spoke and his words came out trembling.

"When?"

"During the fire. It was parked down there," Ethan pointed in front of them. "It pulled away when I ran to the house."

"What kind of car was it?"

Ethan shook his head, "I don't know. It was a black car."

"Like the one at the hut?"

Ethan shook his head, swallowing back the pain. "Nicer. Probably why I didn't notice it then. It blended in with the neighborhood."

"Vargas had a black Mercedez back then, didn't he?"

Ethan tried to recall, but now his mind had become stuck on the image of his house burning.

He began breathing heavier, closing in on hyperventilating. He squeezed his eyes closed, releasing a string of tears that burned his face as they fell. "I don't know."

Ethan forced a breath in, shifting his truck into gear. He pulled away from the memories.

Chapter 25

Ethan and John arrived downtown a little after 11 a.m., found a parking lot near the City/County Building, paid the fee, and turned the ignition off, letting the truck finally rest after a full morning of more output than it had done in years. Ethan could feel the protest of the engine even as it faded before he removed the key.

"I forgot how much I hate driving in the city. And paying for parking," Ethan groaned, shoving his wallet back into his front pocket.

John took a deep inhale through his nostrils. "It smells so beautiful here."

"Beautiful isn't how I'd describe it." Ethan let the smells of the city invade his senses. The exhaust fumes, the tang of metal, and something he couldn't identify offended his nose.

"What's the plan? Are you going to call Grant?"

Ethan adjusted himself in the seat. The metal springs had been pressing into his lower back most of the morning, causing a stiffness that ran up to his shoulders. His legs felt numb, so he stretched them to the back of the underwell. "I was thinking I'd find a quiet spot between here and the office. People are generally more open when they don't have time to plan their answers."

"How do you know he'll be walking through there? Or that he's even working today?"

"Just hoping. If he isn't, then I can call him."

"So, when are we going?"

Ethan opened his door, stepping halfway out. "*We* aren't. For all we know, Vargas may have seen us leave. I want you to stay within eyesight of us, but off to the side. That way, I can focus on the conversation, and you can make sure I'm not an easy target."

"Suppose I see him or one of his goons approaching you, or they decide to just pull up in a car. What am I supposed to do about that?"

"Be vigilant. Yell at me before they get close enough to do anything." Once he and John were both out of the truck, Ethan locked the door. "Did you ever hear back from the P.I.?"

John Waters's head swayed, disappointed, stuffing his hands into his jean's pockets. "Not yet. I'll shoot him a text later."

The wind slapped Ethan's face as he walked. Despite the towering scrapers around him, the wind felt different in the city. Trees were a much better barrier to the cold winds, Ethan had discovered, and the passing cars only added more whips of frosty air as they sped past. Ethan tucked his hands deep into his pocket, clutching his keys as if they held the power of warmth. Each time a dark-colored car drove past, he'd watch it move from the corner of his eye, wondering if it was Vargas—or someone from his crew. The closer Ethan got to Wabash Street the more John fell back.

Wabash Street had no benches or any place for him to stand where he felt he could appear inconspicuous. At the corner of the street sat a Whole Foods, a little further up Alabama Street, which ran perpendicular to Wabash. He decided he would stand outside watching his phone with nothing on it to keep his focus. When Grant walked by, he could spark the conversation without—he hoped—looking too obvious that, that had been his intention all along. He had never been good at this type of thing. That was the main reason he had only ever gone on one stakeout. Of course, once he was appointed the chief prosecutor, he had other people do that.

Ethan noticed John cross Alabama Street at Wabash Street before entering some sort of bicycle shop. From that position, he would likely have a clear view of Ethan on the corner, though Ethan was concerned that he wouldn't be able to see anyone approaching Ethan. Never mind seeing a suspicious car in the mix of all the others. Even if he did, it would be hard for John to get his attention in time for Ethan to react. The creeping sense of suspicion began tugging on the back of his mind again. He tried to contain the nagging notion as well as he could.

Fortunately, he caught sight of the second-hand Armani suit and over-dyed hair coming down the walkway. For a moment, Ethan froze. He hadn't planned how he would engage Grant, standing there now on the corner, it felt odd. He knew if someone had done it to him, he would feel cornered, instantly on guard doing anything he could to get away from the person. Ethan hadn't spoken to Grant since resigning his position, but even before that, most of his conversations had been about work. The few conversations he had with him once Grant took his family's case ended with Ethan storming out of his office, burning over the fact they were no closer to getting Vargas than they ever had been.

Ethan pushed his face back into his phone, deciding to wait until right when Grant passed him before saying anything. However, it was Grant who acknowledged Ethan, which he wasn't sure was better or worse.

"Ethan Barret? Are you back in town? I thought you left?" Grant raised his arms high, wrinkling the Armani coat—which upon closer inspection, Ethan realized, was new and not off-the-rack—and nearly clocking Ethan with his briefcase. He embraced Ethan a little too tightly. "You look damn good."

"Thank you, Grant. So do you."

"I've been meaning to call," Grant said, lowering his head to cover a bit of shame. "We had a lock on Vargas about a month ago."

Ethan hadn't expected the comment. His breath became caught in his throat. "Where... where is he?"

"Walk and talk?"

Ethan didn't respond, he just started walking with Grant. He looked over his shoulder toward the bike shop, slightly relieved to see John exit, following behind a group of teens in an attempt to conceal himself.

"I wish I had better news. Unfortunately, he's back in the wind. No one has seen or heard from him in about three weeks. Even the CIs claim radio silence from him."

Ethan felt himself relax; thankful Grant had started the conversation. "I think I might know where he is."

"Where?" Grant's focus shifted from the sidewalk in front of him to Ethan.

"At my cabin."

"Wait, what?" Grant stopped mid-stride.

"I think. I'm not one hundred percent, but someone has been out there. They even left a news clipping on my porch. Then they left me a SIM card with a bunch of pictures of me. Like he's been following me."

Grant's face showed his clear confusion. "Vargas isn't the type of guy to fuck around. If it were him, I can't imagine he'd do any of that. He'd just put a bullet in your head and call it a day." He started walking again. Ethan followed, keeping stride.

"Unless he wants to make me squirm. I was the only one who'd even gotten close to putting him away. It's always been more personal with me."

Grant sighed. "Our guys have no jurisdiction out there. I can reach out to the local Sheriff or Indiana State Police."

"No," Ethan said quicker than he'd hoped, "Sorry. I just don't want to draw any more attention to myself than I need to. Have you guys gotten a bead on Manuel Rodrigez?"

A snide smirk pulled Grant's lip upward. "Killed in a shootout with the Federales. About six months ago."

"Has Vargas' cartel remained as big as it was a year ago?"

"Your trial did more damage than anticipated. Even without the conviction on Vargas, we ended up taking down a few top guys. With all the uncertainty a lot of the smaller guys defected to other cartels. He cleaned house. A real blood bath from what I've heard."

"When you guys had a pin on him, what was he driving?"

Grant shook his head, stopping at the steps of City Hall, where his office was. "Bastard was smart. He never drove the same thing for more than a couple of days. Never stayed in the same location, either. By the time units came up with a tactical plan, he was gone when they executed them. There's a standing warrant, so if we get word he's here, they can just go. Problem is, we have no say in Chicago or Texas, which have been the other two spots he's been located."

"That doesn't make sense."

"What's that?"

"Why wouldn't he just stay in Mexico? He could do whatever he wanted down there and not have so much heat up his ass."

"Well, he burned a lot of bridges when he got arrested. As I said, your case essentially folded his cartel. Other cartels thought he'd bring heat on them, as well. If he's seen here, he just risks arrest.

If he's spotted down there…" Grant slid his thumb across his neck to paint a more gruesome picture than he thought he could with simple words.

"Hey, I appreciate you talking to me."

"Anytime. You know you can call anytime. We all want to get this bastard as bad as you do."

Ethan smiled, gave a nod of appreciation, then turned to walk back to the car. He saw John leaning against the brick of a building across the street.

"Hey," Grant said, stopping Ethan. "Even if you don't want the bigger departments involved, you need to talk with the local police out there. If it is Vargas, you need all the help you can get."

"Learn what you wanted?" John asked once he got into the truck. He stayed across the street for a time when Ethan started walking back to the car. Ethan had gotten in and turned the heat on full, rubbing his hands together for nearly a minute before John arrived.

"More or less." Ethan looked at John. "Aren't you cold?"

"I was before I got in here. What do you mean, 'more or less.'"

"They had eyes on Vargas a few weeks ago. He's back in the wind. Apparently, his cartel has mostly folded. He's more or less on his own. Grant suggested I contact the local cops."

"Sounds like what I told you, too."

"Yeah. Anyway, if Vargas is trying to settle something, we don't have to worry about a whole army. Just him, maybe one other guy."

"That's comforting."

"It is," Ethan said. He had picked up on the mocking tone in John's delivery but decided to ignore it.

"What I don't get, is why he's got such a hard-on for you."

Ethan grimaced at the image. "What's that supposed to mean?"

"I was just thinking, it's not like you're the first DA to try and put charges on him. He'd always beaten them and went about his life. With you, he loses his mind in open court, then goes after you and everything you love. Why?"

"Maybe he thought I was responsible for his deal being tossed."

John shook his head. "I guess when you're used to believing you're untouchable, something like that would set you off."

"Let's get back. I want to get home before dark. Make sure my house is still standing."

Chapter 26

It was nearly 7 p.m. when Ethan and John returned to the cabin. They had stopped at a small diner they spotted from the highway, barely exiting in time. The food was good, but it had been heavy. Ethan was ready to crawl into bed to catch up on the sleep beckoning him. The sun was already down, but it was the long hours of sitting he accredited to his fatigue. He could spend a whole day chopping wood, hiking the woods, hunting, fishing, or doing chores around the property without feeling tired. He chuckled to himself as he got out of the truck, thinking back to when he first arrived at the cabin. As he began going through the chores on his list to not just make the cabin livable but to live comfortably out here, he would be exhausted nearly all the time. The soreness dug deep into his muscles, sometimes causing cramps in places he had never experienced.

As Ethan walked, he kept his eyes glued to the ground, diligently checking the earth for signs someone had been there. The darkness was thick with the sun setting before 6 p.m. forcing him to squint harder. Trying to focus on the ground with no light to make any sign obvious caused a small headache to punch the front of his head, just behind his eyes. Ethan's neck was already tight like rebar had formed where his scapulae should've been. He decided to relax his eyes, turning his focus to getting inside. Nothing stood out to him anyway. Even on the deck, he saw no obvious sign someone had been there. There was a thick scent of charred wood wafting through the forest, catching his nostrils. He took a deep whiff as he dug for the keys in his pocket. Just behind the smell of charred wood was a chemical smell he couldn't quite identify, but it also wasn't surprising. A lot of people threw trash in the fire pit. It was cheaper than trash collection and easier than driving it into town.

Ethan unlocked the door, flipping the light switch after he entered. John went straight to the couch, collapsing in the spot that had somehow become *his*. Ethan started a fire, rubbing his hands together vigorously, intermittently blowing in them to speed the process.

"Are you going to take Grant's advice?" John asked from the couch, his head tilted over the backrest, his eyes closed.

"About going to the local cops?" Ethan asked, staying close to the stove as the flames began wrapping around the small logs.

John simply nodded. He rolled his head to the left, opening one eye to see Ethan's response.

"I doubt it. If the feds or state guys can't keep a grip on Vargas, the local cops sure can't. They're not equipped to handle someone like him." Ethan finally stood, rubbing his hands over the fire one last time, hoping to carry some of the heat with him back to the couch. "They'll just tell me there's no proof he's anywhere near here. Or that even if he is, there's nothing they can do unless they catch him in the act."

"Even so, if they know there's a chance he's out here, they can call the feds in to monitor your property. They won't just try to catch him on their own."

"It seems like it'll cause more problems than it'd solve."

"What is your deal, man? Why won't you listen to anyone?"

Ethan shifted in discomfort that came from something other than the couch. It came from something he couldn't quite identify. The idea of the FBI or DEA watching over his property unnerved him. It didn't make him feel safe, rather, he felt vulnerable. There was also something a little deeper, something he was almost afraid to speak out loud. The fantasy of finding Vargas in the woods, showing him the justice he knew the legal system never could. He pressed his lips tightly, holding the confession in. Instead, he muttered, "I'm exhausted." Ethan slapped his hands to his knees, standing slower than he had intended, stretching his back to release the knots rapidly forming along his spine. "Let's get some sleep. We can discuss it more in the morning when we're both more clear-headed."

"I can't go to sleep. It's not even eight. You're just trying to avoid this conversation."

"Yes, I am. Good night."

Ethan made his way down the hallway. While he did want to avoid having to explain why he didn't want any outsiders stepping into his situation—at least not the ones he could avoid, unlike John—he also already left himself susceptible by being gone all day. If the FBI, DEA, or any other department stepped in, he would lose all control of the situation. To him, he needed to be at the center of it. He had held onto the delusion living behind a gate would keep his family safe. He grasped at the delusion that being District Attorney meant something, that he would be protected because of the title. He believed the police when they told him they'd find Vargas. He trusted his former colleagues to keep his family's case a priority. In each situation, time after time, he learned no one was looking out for him, his wife, or his daughter. They were dead, and if he let someone else take control, he would be, too.

Ethan stepped into his room, kicking his shoes off to somewhere in the shadows. His rifle was still by the doorframe, so he turned his light on to check it. Satisfied it was loaded, he flipped the switch off. His bed beckoned him from a short distance. Then, a chair to the left, near a window, stole his attention.

Ethan hit the switch again, flooding the room with light once more. In the old rocker was Mary's charred bear. It's one black button-eye staring at him. In the lap of the bear was a manila envelope, his name sprawled across the front in black marker.

The burning in his eyes moved down to his stomach. Ethan didn't notice the pain forming in his jaw from his clenched teeth. He didn't notice his breathing picking up, bringing him dangerously close to hyperventilation. The world around him almost went black, but he held on. It was like he was clinging to a cliff in his mind, his fingertips the only thing keeping him from plummeting.

Finally, he pulled himself up. The world around him became more apparent, allowing him to yank the envelope from the bear. He sat on the edge of the bed, feeling the inside of the envelope, ensuring it wasn't filled with something that could hurt him if he opened it. It felt flat. It felt smooth.

Ethan opened the envelope, looking inside checking for any unidentified powders. Again, it seemed safe. He pulled the contents from the envelope, which in his hands felt like photos.

When they were free from the confines of their packaging, it was confirmed that six 8.5x11-inch photos rested between his thumb and fingers.

The first one was his truck pulling out of the driveway, he assumed from that morning. It looked like it had been taken from a close proximity. Whoever had taken it was likely standing on his property. The following photo was of a burning building. Ethan didn't recognize it. He knew it wasn't his house, from the size of the blaze and because it looked like it was night in the photo. The third photo was Ethan leaving Beaver's, taken from the side of the cabin opposite where John had been. The fourth and fifth photos were also of Ethan. One of him sleeping, taken from outside of his window. The other was of Ethan outside of the drug house, tossing the pistol into the bushes.

He crumbled the contents as tightly as he could. Ethan felt the heat of his rage rush up from his stomach through his arms as he threw the crumbled ball across the room. The secrets were becoming too much to hide. As hard as he'd tried to forget them, as if they'd never happened, they were still coming back.

Chapter 27

Ethan was awakened by a repetitive knock from somewhere in the cabin. He had been sleeping hard and at first, he thought the knocking was a dream. "Come in," he said, thinking John was at the bedroom door. When there was no answer, just the continued knocking, he rolled out of bed. Ethan rushed toward his door, grabbing his rifle before continuing into the living room. John was still asleep, unaware of the endless knocking at the front door.

Ethan kept his voice low when he told John to wake up. John slept on. Ethan noticed the sun was already up, which meant he had slept in. Something he hadn't intended to do, nor was it something he wanted to do. Ethan leaned against the door with his shoulder, his rifle resting across his body with the muzzle aimed toward the door. He twisted the lock pulling the door toward himself, poking his head around to look through the three-inch gap between the door and frame. He moved his finger to the edge of the trigger.

Standing on the other side was a man he didn't recognize. Despite the shirt embroidered with *Police* across his right shoulder and the shiny bronze badge on his left, Ethan was on edge. His finger bounced from the side of the trigger as if arguing with his brain to stay in the ready. The man wore a black baseball cap, reiterating *Police* across the front. A gun was strapped to his hip over his blue jeans. Cuffs dangled on the opposite end. Despite the sun barely climbing the horizon, the man wore sunglasses. His lips were pursed beneath a short brown beard. His face had been carved from stone and showed he had witnessed a great deal of violence. His skin had grown tanned from hours in the sun, which meant he preferred the field to riding a desk.

"Good morning," his voice was low. "I'm Detective Klein, may I come in?"

Ethan examined the badge closer. Then he examined Klein's eyes after he lowered his glasses, slipping the ear hook of his glasses into his shirt just under the top button. Ethan took the rifle into his left hand then leaned it against the wall behind the door. "I'll step outside."

Ethan rounded the door so he could step onto the porch. The cold morning air hit him and he felt ridiculous standing there in shorts, a t-shirt, and barefoot. Even with the wood stove not burning the inside had been much warmer. Suddenly, he was questioning why he didn't just let the detective in.

"What can I do for you?" Ethan asked, wanting to get the conversation over with quickly so he could start the stove.

"What's your name, sir?"

"Do you *need* my name?"

Klein smirked, "I just like to know who I'm talking to."

"With all due respect, you came here. I don't think my name is relevant."

"Is there a reason you don't want to share it?"

Ethan realized if he continued down this path, he could put another target on his back. Klein would be the one aiming for it. "Ethan Barret," he said reluctantly.

"Ethan. I have a cousin named Ethan. Were you home last evening?"

Ethan nodded. "Had to go to Indianapolis yesterday but got home early evening. Then went to bed."

"Do you know your neighbors out to the south?"

Ethan's mind had been racing, only just beginning to slow. He pointed in the direction of Beaver's cabin. "That one?"

"No, over the ridge." Klein reached into his back pocket, where he retrieved a small notebook with a pen clipped to the cover. He flipped it open, clicking the pen ready to write.

Ethan felt pressure building in his stomach, causing a sharp pain to pinch just below the sternum. He hadn't expected the reaction. He didn't know them, not really. But the image of him following them, then holding the two college kids at gunpoint flashed through his mind. He knew he wouldn't be able to explain that. If they had been working with Vargas, he may have shown them the pictures. They could've given them to the police. Him standing outside of the kid's house wiping down a gun.

"No. Not sure I've ever met them. What's this about?"

Klein cleared his throat. "Sometime yesterday, their cabin burned down. One was killed in the fire; the other is at St. Mary's in intensive care."

Ethan's shock was genuine. "Really?"

"Yes. Looks like they were manufacturing methamphetamine," Klein said laconically. "Something sparked, and the whole place went up." He turned his attention to his notepad. "So, you didn't hear or see anything?"

"Must've happened before we got back."

"We?"

Ethan bit at his lip. "My buddy is down here visiting from Indianapolis. He's been here the past few days."

"Mind calling him out here? Maybe he heard something."

Ethan rolled his shoulders. "He went to the city with me. I don't think he would've heard anything if I didn't."

"I'd still like to speak with him," Klein's eyes pierced down. His attempts at intimidation were not as successful as he thought. Ethan had stared into the eyes of ruthless men who would rather kill him than speak to him. Klein's eyes held none of the same violent promises.

Ethan opened his door and leaned in, calling out to John. He wasn't on the couch. Probably in the bathroom. He yelled for John to come outside when he was done.

"That's okay, I can wait. Anyway, what time did you say you came home?"

"I didn't," he said. "But I think it was around seven."

Klein nodded, wrote down Ethan's answer, and then said, "The Fire Department thinks the explosion happened sometime around then. It would've been loud and probably caused a bit of a tremor, too. Are you sure you didn't hear anything?"

"Nope. I was in bed asleep by eight or nine." Ethan heard the bathroom door open from inside.

Suddenly, Klein's attention was stolen from Ethan by a crackling voice coming over the radio strapped to his hip. Ethan hadn't noticed it, despite its blocky appearance. "Klein, we need you back at the scene."

"Ten-Four," he said, speaking into a little device strapped to his shoulder. "I need to get going, but I'd like to talk more with you and your friend." Klein handed Ethan a card from his breast pocket. "If you think of anything, give me a call. I'll stop by again tomorrow."

Ethan took the card, nodding. Klein bound down the two steps of the porch toward his unmarked SUV. The Suburban had been running. Ethan became envious that he was about to feel the warm blast of air in his vehicle. Klein backed the vehicle up and aimed it straight down the drive.

As he began to pull away, John came outside. "Did you ask for me?" His eyes caught the back end of the SUV. "Who was that?"

"The cops."

"The cops? What did they want?"

Ethan turned back into the house; his feet burned from the cold. He started working on the stove to push the cold sting from his flesh.

"Hello?" John's arms were folded across his chest; his back leaned against the closed door.

"Those drug dealer's shack blew up last night. He wanted to know if we saw or heard anything. I told him we hadn't."

"Meth?"

Ethan nodded.

"Probably smoking around the cooking area," John said matter-of-factly. He never practiced criminal law, but the way he spoke made it sound as if it was a circumstance he'd seen a thousand times.

"Probably." Ethan knew that was a likely possibility. But there were other possibilities that were just as likely. They had crossed Vargas somehow, and he made an example out of them. Or he had done it as part of a bigger scheme. He had taken pictures of Ethan outside of their pusher's house, a gun visible in his hands. That tied him to those dealers. If Vargas wanted, he could paint a convincing picture to the police that Ethan had robbed those kids and then torched the dealer's house.

Ethan's heart skipped a beat, making him woozy. The stabbing pain in his gut spread upward into his chest. He had to sit before he passed out.

"Do you think Beaver could've had something to do with it?" John asked, making his way to the couch.

"Why would he do it?"

"He was there, right? Maybe something happened between them,"

Ethan shook his head. "This feels like Vargas. It's his M.O."

"Well, things are escalating fast. With Vargas in the dark, you need to call that cop and tell him to get the feds out here. It's only a matter of time before he comes after you next."

"Then I guess we better find him before then."

Ethan poked the logs in the stove. Movement outside of his window stole his attention. The snow was starting to dance downward toward the earth.

Chapter 28

"Something happened to cause him to get nervous," John offered.

"Or he's just lost all control. He wiped out most of his crew; every other cartel and law enforcement agency has him at the top of their list. He's starting to get on edge."

John shook his head, skeptical. "What doesn't make sense is, if he has that many eyes on him, then why go through so much trouble to show you he can get right next to you without you knowing?"

Ethan had asked himself the same question moments before. He stood from beside the stove when his face became uncomfortably warm, causing sweat to bead under his hairline. "Maybe because getting to me means something more to him."

"More than losing hundreds of millions of dollars? More than staying out of prison?" John walked over to the couch, taking a spot at the end before kicking his feet up onto the table. "Seems to me the payoff isn't worth the risk. If this was just about you, he would've burned your house down like those hillbillies. Or shot you with something stronger than a camera lens."

Ethan put his face in his hands. The burning had subsided from his chest, but it had doubled down in his stomach. He feared he was going to become sick sitting there. The heat from the stove suddenly made it hard to breathe.

"What are you not telling me?"

Ethan took a deep breath. Something under the surface began to boil. "Just drop it."

"You need to start being honest. Why is Vargas going through so much trouble to get at you without making a move? That isn't like him."

"Maybe I was wrong. Maybe it isn't Vargas," Ethan offered, hopeful John would let it drop. He knew he should've known it would never be that easy.

"Okay, then why would *anyone* go through all of this just to see you squirm?"

Ethan felt the boiling inside his stomach rise past his chest to his throat. He bit his lip, swallowing the anger, forcing the shame that replaced it down as well. "I've done things I'm not proud of. When your job is keeping an entire city safe, sometimes you must make deals to serve the greater good. Even if you know it means costing you everything you stand for."

John leaned in, not speaking to make sure he wouldn't interrupt.

When Ethan took his oath, he swore to uphold the law. It was an oath he took seriously. Over the years, though, he saw guilty men and women walk free, sometimes from technicalities, sometimes from lack of evidence, but mostly from scared witnesses too frightened to speak. He watched as people would visit the courtroom as frequently as he went to the grocery store. Each time, the charges became more serious. He saw murderers get off as if they had simply run a red light. He was tired of it. One day, Mary would be out in the world on her own, and she would have to witness the darkest parts of it. God forbid, she would experience it in all its horrendous reality. Ethan had never imagined that by trying to make a safer world for his daughter, the darkness he tried to protect her from would wind up right on his front step. That she would have to experience it most intimately.

"There was more to the deal with Vargas than anyone else knew," Ethan said aloud.

"What was that, exactly?"

"On paper, it would've been ten years in federal prison, then ten years on probation."

John nodded. "I remember the judge threw it out."

"Right," Ethan began to rock on the couch, the burning in his stomach was not getting better. "Vargas gave me five million cash to make sure he would serve time in Terre Haute." Ethan paused, swallowed the painfulness of his naïveté back then. "He said medium security where he had a lot of associates. He could continue running his cartel from there and have the security to back his move. He would've been out in five, at most."

"He gave you five million but not to stay out of prison?"

"I didn't know until later that he was going to organize a rescue. The bus would've taken 65 North from downtown to Terre Haute. If the ambush happened on the highway, they could've gone in any direction before backup arrived. Hide a second vehicle on one of the country roads nearby. He could've gotten away clean. A lot easier to pull off headed to a medium-security facility than a maximum one. That's why he needed me to make the deal. He played me."

"Why would you agree to that anyway?"

Ethan lowered his head as the shame nearly suffocated him. He stammered as he answered, "I made him promise to keep his runs out of Indiana. If he came back, he would get life."

John leaned closer. He felt like a towering force next to Ethan, who felt as though he were shrinking.

"Once the deal was turned down, he knew he would be restricted from outside contact and not be told where he was going until the transfer was arranged. He wouldn't have been able to contact anyone to change the plans. He blamed me because I promised it would happen."

"Why didn't he just tell the judge about the money? That would've fucked your whole life up."

"Well," Ethan choked out, "He did a pretty good job of that without telling anyone anything."

John leaned back, giving Ethan some room. He no longer felt suffocated, but the rock in his throat refused to budge. "Obviously, you couldn't say anything."

Ethan shook his head in acknowledgment. "Obviously."

"Did Kristina know?"

Ethan brought his eyes up. "No. I've never told anyone this," the tears he had been fighting back broke over the edge of his eyes. His voice dropped, trembling as he spoke. "She was going to leave me. I think part of me also took the money so I could stop working so much. I could give more of myself to my family."

"Why didn't you ever tell me?"

"Not something you want to share with the world. That I had neglected my family so severely my wife was ready to leave."

"What happened to the money after all of that?"

"It's somewhere safe. I don't feel right using it, but I can't just turn it in. I certainly can't give it back."

"How'd he get it to you?"

"I rented a boat on Morse Reservoir. I met one of his guys on the lake and he gave me a bag with all the money. The next morning, I started drafting the plea deal. That afternoon, everything fell apart."

"That's not good, Ethan."

"Don't you think I know that?" Ethan screamed out. "If I hadn't agreed to his deal, my family would still be here! They're dead because of *me*."

John shook his head. "They're dead because of Vargas. You could never have known what would happen."

"That's bullshit. I should've known nothing good would've come from it. I should've known once the judge threw the deal out, I was finished." Ethan ran the back of his hand across his face to wipe the tears. "I wish he'd just told the judge I'd taken the bribe. At least then, my family would still be here."

"You don't know that," John told him.

"That's why I don't want the feds involved. I want to be the one to take him down. I don't want this to end until one or the other of us is dead."

John took a deep breath. He moved his hands to his knees as leverage to help him stand. "I'm going to step outside for some fresh air. That's a lot to process." John removed his phone from his pocket, tossing it onto the couch beside Ethan. "So you know I'm not out there calling anyone."

A sudden wave of relief hit Ethan. It was as if a pressure valve had been twisted, releasing everything that had been building up inside of him. His body suddenly felt weak as the tension in his muscles left. "I know."

❦

From the window, Ethan could see John sitting by the firepit. He was bundled up in a coat, his hands deep in his pockets as thick snowflakes fluttered down on top of him... He seemed to be staring off into the woods, presumably trying to process the new information. He had known Ethan his entire career. Ethan had always been ethical, a pursuer of justice, believing no man was above the law. Ethan couldn't begin to guess how betrayed John felt learning everything Ethan stood for had such a low price. Or, that it had a price at all. It had all become so tiring. Justice was becoming a losing battle. No matter how many criminals he put away, three more popped up. More violent, more ruthless, and with less morals—or at least the flawed concept of morals. Vargas had been one of the worst. Ethan just wanted him gone. Doing so, he knew, meant doing something immoral. If he had taken him to trial, it was only a 50/50 chance he would've seen any actual jail time. He was lucky he had convinced Vargas he would lose a trial. Otherwise, Vargas would've walked out free. He knew Vargas would continue to poison the streets of his city, killing innocent people with his drugs and the inherent violence that came with doing business. He did what he thought he had to do to stop it. He should've known there was no way to stop it. There was only a speed bump in the process.

Ethan pulled himself from the window. He went to the fridge, where he pulled a topographical map he had placed under a magnet. He used the map to track hunting lines, where cameras had been placed, and where he had seen deer. Now, he needed it to track Vargas. He guessed if he had been at the motel, he wouldn't be going back there. He certainly couldn't go back to the shed. However, the public land around them offered a lot of concealment. He was also confident that if they were cooking meth as well as moving drugs through their shack, they probably had another building somewhere in the woods that couldn't be traced back to them. Vargas never operated without multiple places to go to if any heat came his way. Ethan hadn't explored much of the woods beyond his property line and some portions of the public land that separated his property from Beaver's.

The map covered his property primarily but also included a sliver of Beaver's, as well as the public section of land beyond the ridge toward the property of the pushers. From the topographical map, he could tell the terrain on his property was mostly flat. Once at the ridge moving beyond the now burned-down shack, the terrain was much hillier. Elevation changes of 300 feet or more surrounded the area. Vargas made a fortune smuggling, so Ethan knew he would be avoiding the higher elevations. It made it easier for any drones flying overhead to spot his heat signature, especially as the temperatures continued to drop. The fresh falling snow would make his body heat, plus the fires he would need to stay warm, light up like a Christmas tree on the thermals.

Ethan knew there were no caves in the area for him to hunker down in to conceal body heat or movement. That left the lower valleys between the towering hills where his body heat would be slightly shielded by the treetops, especially now that they were being coated with snowfall. Based on the map, Mark and Gus's property reached just to the opposite side of the ridge, then out for five acres. It went back before wrapping around like a big square. Fifteen total acres, with about five acres separating the three neighbors' property lines. The land to the west, behind Beaver's property line, looked to be state land, but it had been color-coded differently than the designated public land. It was hilly, but there was one section of lowland between two large hills. Ethan grabbed a marker that had been clipped to the top of the map, circling the section twice. It was the most likely place for Vargas to hide out until he either decided to jump ship or confront Ethan.

The area would be shielded from drones with tall, thick trees—now covered in a quarter inch of snow and counting—provided water from the creek, and if Vargas walked the valley four miles south, he would eventually come to a road. He could hitchhike out or have someone pick him up from there. Ethan did a quick measurement, calculating that it was five miles from his cabin. He assumed he could get there in a little over ninety minutes with the snowfall. Except, the snow showed no signs of slowing down. It could get much worse, making travel that much more difficult.

Plus, he thought to himself, what was he going to do if Vargas was there? Hunt him down like a deer? It would be the easiest method. Sit tucked away behind a tree fifty yards away, one shot would end the whole thing. But shooting a man, even an evil, vile man like Vargas was not the same thing as shooting a deer. If he confronted Vargas, he could wait for him to pull his gun. That would be clear-cut self-defense. He could achieve the same result without the guilt, which he had in spades over other decisions he had made in his life.

Ethan folded the map, putting it into his back pocket before heading back to his room. He went into the closet, pulling on a pair of long johns followed by jeans. He slid on his boots, a thick sweater, topped with his hunting jacket. He stopped, looking at the bear he had left in the chair the night before. Then, he went to the front door to retrieve his rifle. He and John had a long walk ahead of them.

Chapter 29

John came out of the cabin ten minutes later in several more layers than what he went in with. "This must be the worst idea you've ever come up with. If you think he's there, why not just tell the police? It keeps us warm while at the same time getting him into the cell he belongs in. You haven't spent the money. At this point, it's your word against his. I don't think there's a cop out there who'd doubt you."

"Even if all that is true, he's already on edge. Which means he'll be making his move soon. If the cops go in, they'll go in with a small army, choppers, drones, all of it. If he gets spooked, we have no idea where he'll end up. Then I'm spending the rest of my life looking over my shoulder." Ethan slung his rifle over his shoulder, locking his door. "If we go, we can maybe catch him off guard. I can make sure I can actually start over. Like I've been trying to for the past year."

"Maybe you should ask Beaver to go with you. He'd be more useful to you than I will be."

"If you're scared, you can stay here." Ethan descended the steps of his porch, rounding the eastern side of the house. The wind gathered his hair as it collected large flakes, chilling his scalp. He pulled a beanie from his coat pocket, tugging it down to just over his eyes. The snow nearly reached the vamp of his boots. There was no sign of slowing down. He guessed by the time they returned, there would be at least four to six inches of snow on the ground.

"Of course I'm scared. Vargas is a known murderer who doesn't give a damn about your life or mine. We are going into the woods with no backup, no one knows we're out there, who knows how far the nearest hospital is—not to mention how we'd get there if we needed to—and all you have is a hunting rifle." John picked up his pace to stay beside Ethan. "I can't very well let you go out there alone. But I'm also realistic. I'm not going to be much help to you out there. Not like he would be."

"The man's got his own things to worry about. I don't need to go dragging him into my mess."

"Just tell him you found the trespasser. He'll be more than happy to go face-off with him, too."

"Relax, we don't even know if he's out there. It's just a hunch. We might just be going for a nice walk."

As they reached the ridge, Ethan turned right so they could walk around it, passing the shortest part of the hill. Along the bottom of the ridge, Ethan stuck his arm out to stop John. In the snow was a fresh track of a boot, slightly smaller than Ethan's. One track was flat, one slightly behind it to the left was only the toe box, a small indent between the two.

"Someone was here kneeling," Ethan said, kneeling himself. He scanned the area, instantly finding footprints leading around the ridge in the direction they were heading, back into the woods. "They've been here recently."

"Recently enough to see us coming up here?"

Ethan shrugged, unsure. "Maybe."

"Then they might know we're headed out looking for them. Takes away the element of surprise."

Ethan sighed. "Yeah. Unless it was the cops extending their search."

"Into your property?"

"I guess you're right," Ethan conceded. You go back to the cabin," he said, grabbing his key from his pocket and handing it to John.

"Where are you going?"

"I'm going to take someone else's advice for once. I'll go to Beaver's. I'll see if he'll go up there with me. We can hit it from a better angle if we go through his property, and it'll be nice to have another shooter out there if Vargas did see us coming up this way."

"Do you have any whiskey?"

"Have at it. It's in the fridge. If you don't hear from me in three hours, call the police. Tell them we're in the valley back here."

"Be safe."

"I'll do my best."

✤

By the time Ethan reached Beaver's cabin, the cold was penetrating his bones. He let out an audible exhalation of relief when he saw the smoke billowing out of the chimney. He could imagine the warmth washing over him—assuming Beaver would let him in. Ethan was sure the police had paid a visit to Beaver about the shack burning down. Since he had been there, Ethan didn't know if the police had anything that tied him to the place. Or if Beaver would've told on himself somehow. For all he knew, they had dragged him to the station for hours of repeated questions. Of course, depending on how destructive the fire had been, any evidence of Beaver being there may've been destroyed. Ethan couldn't be sure. There was enough left over for them to decide they were cooking meth, but he wasn't a fire expert. Or a drug expert, for that matter.

He rounded the house, climbing the steps to find the door opening just as he was about to knock.

"I think I've seen you more this week than the whole last year combined," Beaver said flatly. He stepped to the side, extending his arm to the interior of his house, welcoming Ethan inside.

Ethan didn't stop to talk. He went right inside, conveniently placing himself near the stove. The warmth was just as soothing as he'd imagined. "Sorry to keep popping in on you," he said. "I saw our trespasser. I think I know where he went. I was going to see if I could catch him off guard. I wanted to see if you'd like to tag along?"

"Hell yes," Beaver growled. His eyes showed signs of eagerness, countered by the harshness in his voice. Then, it dawned on Ethan that the eagerness may be for bloodshed. "That bastard's probably the one who burned down that cabin round the way."

"You heard about that?" Ethan tried to sound surprised, though he didn't know why.

"Cops showed up early this mornin' askin' if I saw anything. I told them no, on account, I don't just go givin' them information on stuff that ain't their business."

"Arson is their business, isn't it?"

Beaver's eyes narrowed. "Nothin' that happens out here is their business. You'd be wise to keep that in mind."

"I will," Ethan said, suddenly feeling uneasy.

"I'll go get layered up."

By the time they reached the ridge again, the snow had intensified. It was coming down so hard that when Ethan went to show Beaver the sign of someone kneeling at the bottom of the ridge, the tracks were nearly covered, leaving only small indents. Ethan followed Beaver around the ridge to the mouth of the valley.

"Why do you suppose this fella got such an itch for you?" Beaver asked, breaking what had mostly been a silent walk.

"What makes you ask that?"

"When I saw him, he was lookin' out toward your lot. Them signs back there looks like he was at it again. You told me you caught someone creepin' around on your property. Seems like he has a lot more interest in your space than just poaching a few deer."

"Maybe he's working for your buddies," Ethan nearly choked on the words as they came out. He hadn't meant to say them out loud.

A crooked smile tilted Beaver's beard on one side. "I knew I saw you out there the other day."

Ethan's grip on his rifle tightened reflexively. He figured if he had to, he could pull it around from his shoulder and fire a quick shot.

"Ease up there, boy. If I was all that worked up about it, I'd have done somethin' about it the day you were diggin' through my drawers."

Ethan's grip didn't ease up. "How'd you know I was in there?"

"When you ain't open a drawer in a decade, you notice when it's been opened. Since you so happened to be knockin' on my door two seconds later, it wasn't all that hard to figure."

"I probably could've handled it differently," Ethan admitted, his eyes glued on Beaver, watching for any sudden movements. He allowed himself to slow a step behind, but Beaver matched his pace to keep them side-by-side.

"Did you find what you was lookin' for?" Beaver looked at Ethan, perhaps searching for the answer in his eyes rather than whatever he might say.

"No. I got that when you told me your name. What I'd like to know though, is why were you over there if you hated them so much?"

Beaver let out a bubbled chuckle. "I never said I hated them. I said, 'Watch out for them.'"

"Because you didn't want me to know you were out there moving drugs?"

"Boy, get your head out of your ass. I wasn't movin' a thing. I didn't like what they were doin', but I understood it. Money's tight for everyone these days. I went by there time from time to make sure they didn't start getting' too loose. I didn't want them bringin' no trouble our way."

"What kind of trouble?" Ethan asked, curious about what past he had been hiding from.

"The kind they found. We got a good, quiet life out here in these woods. The last thing we want is a pissing battle between some fools who get in deeper than they should." Beaver turned his eyes back toward Ethan again. "You know a little about the outcome of somethin' like that, right?"

Ethan clenched his jaw, feeling the tightness spread through his cheeks up into his ears. "You know about my past," Ethan said matter-of-factly.

"When the DA's family is burned, ain't no way you don't hear about it. I don't know much of what's goin' on in the world, but I hear the big things."

"That's why you made it a point to meet me and help me when I first moved out here," Ethan's grip on his rifle finally loosened.

"It was a double-edged situation. I wanted to make sure you wasn't bringin' no trouble out here with you, but also I know what it's like to need to start over. I was trained to live off the land. I suspected you wasn't."

"So, what were you starting over from?"

Beaver shook his head, "We aren't that close."

"You want to trust your neighbor, right? Well, so do I."

Beaver eyed Ethan for a moment. "I had a house with my wife in the suburbs, on account she liked people. Well, she got really sick. Doctors couldn't figure out what from, but she kept on getting' worse and worse until she just couldn't fight anymore. I was outside one day a couple of weeks or so after she passed. Kids came out lookin' through her things, fightin' over who got what. Made me sick." Ethan could hear the emotion welling in Beaver's throat. He knew the loss he was feeling. "I stepped outside to get a break. My neighbor was mowin'. He hit a rock or something. Sent the darn thing flyin' into my yard. Hit my wife's car, shatterin' her window."

Beaver let out another raspy chuckle, except this time Ethan doubted it was from amusement. "I jumped that fence and beat the man senseless. Did about a year in jail and no one in my family came to visit. When I got out, an Army buddy of mine said he was sellin' his cabin. Well, I jumped on it. Never been back since."

"I'm sorry to hear about your wife. It's not easy losing someone, especially the person you planned to grow old with."

Beaver sniffed hard before clearing his throat. "I wasn't always a nice man. I guess in a lot of ways, I still ain't. I just want a quiet life, and I'll be damned if I let anyone get between that and me. So when I found out what them boys was doin' I decided I'd stop in every so often to make sure they weren't getting' too sloppy."

"Why not just report them?"

"Wouldn't do no good. Cops out here ain't crooked, but they ain't exactly equipped to deal with that sort of operation either."

"Were they working with the cartels?"

Beaver shrugged, ducking under a low branch as they entered the last quarter mile of the valley before reaching where Ethan suspected Vargas may have been. "Hell if I know. Didn't seem like they were that organized. I think if they were workin' with them fellas, they'd have to have a tighter ship."

"I think the guy who's been watching me is the man who killed my family."

Beaver stopped, facing Ethan. His eyes were narrow. "Why you say that?"

"Let's just say, he's made it a point to know this is personal for him."

Beaver nodded as if that told him everything, when in fact it told him nothing. "Then I guess if it's him we find out in the valley, we put 'im down." He turned and continued walking.

Chapter 30

Once they reached the point in the valley that would round the bend to the right, Beaver pointed to the left, an expression Ethan took to mean he was supposed to go up the left portion of the valley. The trees were bigger on the rises of either side, providing more cover as well as concealment. They could stay low behind them continuing toward the bend. Just on the other side. Ethan watched Beaver navigate to the correct ridge Ethan suspected Vargas's camp to be before finding his path, made more difficult by the deepening snow.

Ethan leaned against the thick trees as he walked. The angle of the hill mixed with the five inches of snow made it almost impossible for him to find his footing. Every other step felt like the one that would send him tumbling back into the valley. Fortunately, they didn't need to go far. Thirty feet from where Ethan and Beaver broke from the valley into the woods, they stopped gain.

Ethan could see the encampment. A tent took up most of the valley floor, seven feet across, making the tent close to six feet long. It looked to be just as wide. It even had a metal pipe coming through the center, which Ethan recognized as a camp stove. The top had been layered with a camouflaged tarp in the areas surrounding the chimney. The corners of it poked underneath the snow.

Ethan's disappointment bubbled in his chest as it deflated at seeing the camp. The top was covered in snow. Which told Ethan that no one had been at the camp since the snow had started. If they had, they would have either brushed off the snow or been running a fire to warm the tent. The lack of smoke and the mounting snow on top told Ethan neither was happening. Beaver must've noticed it too because he emerged from the woods opposite Ethan, his rifle raised to eye level, approaching the tent.

Ethan grabbed a tree with his left hand for stability, raising the rifle with his right as best he could. Once in the valley, he fell behind Beaver and approached the tent.

The valley floor was nothing but snow, telling Ethan no one had come or gone since it had started. Beaver stuck the barrel of his rifle to the entrance of the tent, giving Ethan a nod. Ethan shook his head persistently, but Beaver's narrowed eyes told him he was going to be the one to open it.

Ethan took a grip on the cord lock at the top, flipped it through the string, then stepped back. When no sound came from inside, he did the same with the middle and then the bottom before pulling the cover back. Beaver stormed inside before Ethan had time to say or do anything. Out of pure reflex, he followed Beaver in. The tent, as he suspected, was empty. The cot near the stove—which had been cold to the touch—was layered with blankets. A bag of clothes rested at the foot of the cot; a black Beretta 9 mm rested in the center of it. Ethan took a step closer to examine the firearm. Gold vines had been laser etched on the slide, flowing back to the grip where they continued down, wrapping the grip to the base.

"Nice piece," Beaver commented.

"It's Vargas's. I recognize it from the evidence report."

"How'd he get it back?"

Ethan picked it up and examined it closer. "He might not have. He has enough money to get another one if he wanted to."

"Seems odd he'd leave it here."

"Yeah, it does," Ethan agreed. "Even if he went to the motel knowing the storm was headed in, he would've taken this."

"Think he got spooked by all the police snooping around 'bout that fire? One hint of them could send him runnin'."

Ethan shook his head. "There'd be no reason for them to come searching this far down the valley. The storm probably drove him out for the night, but I doubt he's gone."

"Well, that's a shame. Means the boy will be back to cause some trouble." Beaver grabbed the gun in Ethan's hand and took it, sliding it into his pack. "Guess we better not make it any easier for him than we need to."

"We better get back before we get snowed in," Ethan said, noticing the snow looked to be picking up outside of the tent. He dreaded going back out into the cold, but the promise of dark liquor and a warm fire was a good motivator. Though Ethan's mind raced as he wondered where Vargas had slipped off to. His mind then went to John, who had walked back to the cabin alone and was there alone now. Vargas could've doubled back, leaving John vulnerable.

"Do you think the cops are still at the shack investigating? Or do you think the snow has slowed them down?"

Beaver gave Ethan a questioning look. "I wouldn't know nothin' 'bout that. I suspect if they start something, they finish it. But wasn't really a whole lot of building to dig through."

"I'd just feel better knowing Vargas would have them dangling over his head."

Beaver nodded his sympathy. "Well, you just holler out your front door and I'll come runnin'."

"Thank you, Beaver. I appreciate everything you've done for me."

"I ain't done nothin' yet."

Chapter 31

Ethan waved his farewell to Beaver when they began heading in opposite directions. He could see his truck nearly buried under the thick snow behind his cabin. He suddenly regretted parking it there, knowing now, he would have to wait until the snow melted over the next few days before he could get it out. But the muddied ground would come with its own set of challenges.

Ethan was at the back of his property when he saw boot tracks in the snow. They seemed to zig-zag over the property near the cabin. The indents were fresh, and deep despite the rapidly falling snow. He didn't think they were John's. He would've had no reason to be walking around the outside of the cabin, from one window to the next.

Ethan brought his rifle up, pointing forward while his eyes scanned the wood line and the front corner of the house, where someone could catch him by surprise. As he approached the front of the cabin, he saw a black SUV where his truck normally sat. A man leaned against it. His arms crossed as his jaws eagerly worked a piece of gum. It took a moment for Ethan to register the face, and then he recognized the man as Detective Klein. He breathed a sigh of relief, which was short-lived. There was no reason for him to be back.

Ethan put the rifle over his shoulder and continued past the house toward the detective, hoping he hadn't noticed Ethan's rifle pointed in his direction.

"Didn't expect to see you back here," Ethan called out when he passed the porch. In the clearing that had become the parking area, the wind whipped. He wondered how long Klein had been standing there. If it had been more than a minute or two, the man was a glutton for punishment.

"Had some interesting developments," he called back as Ethan continued to close the distance.

"Was that you who left all the tracks around my cabin?"

"It was," he confirmed. Then he eyed the rifle. "Not a good day to go hunting."

Ethan nodded, clutching the sling of his rifle a little tighter. "Yeah, it was pretty slow."

"Mind if we head inside? It's a little cold out here."

"Did you knock when you got here? My buddy should be inside," as the words left his mouth, he realized he hadn't noticed any smoke billowing out of the chimney.

"Mmhmm, no answer."

"How long have you been here?"

"Five minutes, if that."

Ethan waved Klein to follow him as he led the way to the door. It was unlocked. Ethan went inside, placing his rifle by the door. His key was on the counter, which he retrieved. "John," he called out. There was no response. He noticed the wood stove was not lit.

"Everything all right?" Klein asked.

"He should be here," Ethan nearly buckled with the knot twisting in his stomach. "Since you're here, I'd like to file a missing person report."

Klein retrieved his notepad with a pen tucked into the spiral binding. "I'll jot his name down. It's too soon to file a report, but you can call me in a couple of days and I'll file it."

"He said he was coming back here; he's not here. Isn't that the definition of *missing*?"

"Look, I assume he's a grown man. He could've gone into town, gone back home, or gone for a walk. Besides, we are bogged down with what's happening on the other side of the ridge right now."

"Some meth cooks blow up their cabin and that's more important than a missing person?"

Klein slid the notepad back into his pocket. "If that's all it was, then no. But a lot has happened since we spoke earlier this morning."

"What could've happened that makes it more important?" Ethan could feel his fists clenching. He bit down on the back of his bottom lip to displace the tension, which only barely helped.

"I'm not saying it's *more* important. Just that currently, all resources are being put into that investigation, and you don't even know if your friend is actually missing. But over there, not only do we have a major manufacturing and distribution of drugs going on, but we discovered a body."

Ethan's throat tightened more. He swallowed hard to prevent his stomach from revolting. "In the burn site?"

Klein shook his head, his eyes glued to Ethan. "Behind the house in a shallow grave. The dogs sniffed it out. Luckily, they found it before the snow got too bad. The guy had been killed and probably buried around the same time as the fire started."

"Who was it?"

"Your friend, Angel Vargas."

Ethan's heart felt like it stopped. "What's that supposed to mean?"

"I ran a check on you after we spoke this morning—standard procedure. Do you believe in coincidences, Mr. Barret?"

"I... I guess so."

"I don't. Never have. I find it quite interesting that a drug dealer burns down your house, tragically with your family inside. The next year, some drug dealer's shack is burned down and the man suspected in your case is found in a shallow grave less than twenty feet away."

"Well... I... I heard that Vargas had made a lot of enemies back home. He is probably on the hit list of dozens of capable people."

Klein nodded in agreement. "Probably. But you're the only one we know who lives on the other side of the ridge from where it all went down. Conveniently, you say you weren't home at the time of the fire. Like I said, Mr. Barret, I don't believe in coincidence."

"They could've been the ones who killed Vargas. They go inside to cook their next batch, someone lights up a cigarette, and the whole place goes up."

Klein pointed a finger at Ethan as if the puzzle had been solved. "I like that theory. It fits everything. Except for one detail."

"What's that?"

"An accelerant was used in the back of the house. It's most likely gasoline. Nothing special about gas being used, but the location is the same as in your case as well."

Ethan's thoughts went back to John. Ethan grew more concerned than he had been when he found the house empty. "Whoever is responsible is probably the same person who took John. If you'd get your head out of your ass and find him, you'd probably find whoever is responsible. Instead, you're so focused on pointing your finger at me, that you're going to get him killed!"

"I'm going to need you to calm down, Mr. Barret. If he doesn't show up in a couple of days, we'll start an investigation. Maybe even send the dogs out here to sniff around."

Ethan was biting on his lip to the point a metallic tang hit the tip of his tongue. "Are you suggesting I had something to do with his disappearance?"

"I'm simply saying we will make sure all bases are covered."

"If Vargas was a loose end, then someone above him was behind the hit on my family. Also, behind the fire out here and Vargas's murder."

"We will be checking into all of that, trust me."

"I think you should go now. I may not practice law anymore, but I'm still aware of my rights. If you have anything else to say to me, you can call me. I'll be busy doing your job though, so I may not be available."

"Just make sure you don't drift too far from here," Klein growled as he let himself out.

When he was alone, Ethan started a fire in the stove to warm himself. The air inside the cabin was only slightly warmer than outside. The thoughts racing through his mind were indecipherable from one to the next. Either someone was setting him up, everything had been a coincidence, or someone was targeting him for something else. Either way, he had been wrong the whole time.

All of that, though, took a backseat to the dominating thought. Where had John gone? Where would he even start to look? He could've been taken anywhere by anyone.

Chapter 32

Once Ethan felt warm again, he went to the kitchen. He grabbed his flashlight, flipped the switch to check the battery, and then stuffed it into his pocket. Then he grabbed his binoculars, pulling them over his neck to lie on his chest. Ethan grabbed his rifle, slinging it over his shoulder before stepping outside and locking the door behind him. He looked out to the driveway, noticing John's car was still there. He had been so focused on Klein leaning against his, he hadn't thought to look at John's. He just suspected it was there, and since nothing stood out to him more than Klein being there, the idea to verify it hadn't moved never crossed his mind. Now, it didn't matter. Wherever John had gone—or been taken— didn't involve his vehicle.

The sun was beginning to set. Just enough light cast over the treetops and reflected from the snow's surface he could see his driveway clearly. Since the snow had stopped thirty minutes before, any tracks that had been left within the past couple of hours would be noticeable. Ethan started with the drive, which showcased one distinct set of tracks, which he knew were Detective Klein's. The thick tire marks distinctly belonging to an SUV. Klein had even driven closely over the same path to leave as he did when he arrived, making it that much easier to spot.

Between the heavy snow and winds, most of the foot traffic leading up to the cabin, particularly on the porch, was long gone. A few prints remained in the yard, marked by nearly indistinct indents of the snow where Ethan and Klein had walked up to the house, vanishing halfway between the driveway and the porch.

Ethan didn't think it would make sense for John to walk off into the woods on his own. He had already gotten lost once. Attempting to go out on his own in the middle of a heavy snowstorm was idiotic, and not something John would've risked. But if someone had come for him, they would be just as foolish. If they had come in on some sort of ATV, Ethan suspected he would've seen some tracks. However, three hours had passed from when Ethan sent John back and he returned. A lot of time for someone to come take John while the snowfall covered any trace of them being there.

Ethan decided the only chance he would have was to ask Beaver. He hated the idea of burdening the man any further. Of course, he reasoned, he only needed to ask his advice. He didn't need him to tag along this time. In fact, there may not be anywhere to tag along to. Ethan bit at his lips again, desperate to suppress the warming feeling in the pit of his stomach. He hated the feeling of losing control. What he hated most of all was knowing if he had answered his phone just once a few days ago, much of this could've been avoided.

He walked up Beaver's driveway, pleased to smell the burning wood from the stove. It was strong with plumes of smoke wafting from the chimney, which meant the fire was strong. It was fresh. Ethan bound up the steps, his toes losing feeling after the quarter-mile hike through ankle-deep snow. Ethan knew the weather would take a turn in the coming days, causing most of the snow to melt. For now, though, it was cold and unforgiving.

Ethan gave a solid knock on the door. After a moment of rustling from inside, the door opened wide. Beaver had a cigar hanging between the part in his white beard. "I didn't expect to see you again so soon."

Ethan followed Beaver into the cabin, sitting in an open chair near the wood stove to thaw his feet. "A lot's happened since then."

Beaver gave him an unnerved look.

"That detective was at my cabin waiting for me when I got back. The guy we were looking for was murdered around the same time the house burned. They think I might've had something to do with it."

Beaver nodded, unfazed. "Makes sense."

"Well, that's not even the biggest problem. I've had a buddy staying with me for the past few days. He was gone when I got back, but his car was still parked in my driveway. I don't have any way of knowing what happened, and I'm concerned. The detective blew me off when I asked to file a report."

Beaver nodded. "Do you think he just walked off? Or do you think it has somethin' to do with what happened to them boys over the ridge?"

"I don't think he went off in the woods on his own if that's what you're asking. He's not that stupid."

"What do you need from me?" Beaver brought down a bottle of Jack Daniels from a cupboard twisting the lid as he did. He took a heavy swig from the top, extending it out to Ethan. Ethan shook his head.

"I'm thinking they took him alive. There wasn't a struggle. They didn't leave a body. Is there anywhere around here they could've taken him to hold him until they got to me?"

Beaver thought for only a moment. "There's a cabin about two miles down from here. Been empty as long as I've been here. Probably not in good shape, but ain't nowhere else I can think of."

"Who all knows about it?"

Beaver shrugged. "I guess anyone who has one of them phone apps. If they were lookin' at the lay of the land to get a good idea of the terrain, they'd have seen the overgrowth of the road and probably the cabin, too."

"There's nowhere else they might've taken him?"

"Not that's private. I think all the other cabins and houses out here have folks livin' in 'em."

"What about Mark and Gus? Anyone they might've associated with that would want them dead and John just got caught in the crossfire?"

Beaver scratched his beard searching for an answer. "I don't know who all they had business with. But no matter who it was, I can't see no one going out to your place to take your friend over it. Especially with them already dealt with."

Ethan's mind went to the two college kids. But the idea quickly faded as the image of their terrified faces crept into his memory. They wouldn't have had the guts to pull off any of this. An associate of Vargas, perhaps, but Ethan wasn't sure how he or John would fall into their plan of retribution.

"You tried callin' the man?"

Ethan bit his lip again, wincing at the pain of the now raw spot he had created. "I didn't think about that."

"I say try that, if you don't get no answer then consider lookin' in that old cabin. But even then, might be best to hold up two days, then let the police go search for 'im."

"I can't wait that long. If something happens to him, I'll never be able to live with myself. I let my family down. I can't let him down, too."

Beaver shrugged. "Suit yourself. Just swing by here when you make your decision and I'll tag along."

"I can't ask you to do that."

Beaver let out a wet chuckle. "This the most excitement my old ass has seen in a while. Beats anything else I had goin' on."

"I appreciate that. I'll go back home to call him. Hopefully, he answers and it's all just a big overreaction." Ethan could feel it wasn't. Someone had gotten John out of the cabin. What if they had been in there waiting? When John came back, they could've ambushed him, leaving no time to react. That would explain why there hadn't been any sign of an altercation. Also, how they got him out of the cabin in the first place.

"Keep me in the loop," Beaver said, following Ethan to the front door.

"I will," Ethan lied. He knew he wouldn't call on Beaver unless he had to. He'd disrupted the man's life enough.

❦

Ethan knew by the time he got to the vacant cabin the sun would be well below the horizon. He would have nothing but the moon to guide him. If someone was in the cabin, he didn't want to risk using the flashlight. It would tell them exactly where he was, which was the last thing he needed. He had already talked himself out of waiting until morning. If John was there, either by force or because he had somehow gotten lost, he didn't want him there any longer than he already had been.

Ethan decided to leave the main road to enter the woods on the right side. He knew the land would be more even, so even with the snow he would remain on relatively stable footing. The left side had a slight grade, which would increase his likelihood of either falling or creating noise. Ethan continued along his path for fifty yards before stopping at a log. He could see the silhouette of the cabin against the backdrop of snow-covered trees.

The siding of the cabin appeared to be in relatively good condition—all things considered. However, the roof appeared to be sagging in the middle, which caused the far walls to bow inward. The right end of the house had begun to sink into the earth, at some point being reinforced by large stones. He could see tracks of some sort of vehicle near the house, though from his position, it was impossible to tell what had caused them. He raised his binoculars from their resting place at his chest. Ethan peered through the eyepieces to the cabin. The magnification offered little assistance, certainly not what he had hoped for. The tracks still only looked like lines in the glowing snow. The house still looked blacked out in the night. However, he was able to confirm that no lights were on inside. He went back and forth in his mind for a moment on whether it was worth the risk to go in. If someone was staying there, they could return any moment. If the house didn't cave in first. But the deciding factor, the thought that pushed him from his place behind the log and toward the house, was that if there was any chance John was inside, he needed to check.

Ethan made it a point to stay near the thicker parts of the underbrush and fallen logs, limiting his tracks. In places where he had no choice but to step in the undisturbed snow, he would brush the surrounding snow back into his track.

Ethan kneeled behind a fallen log, propped up by a large boulder that had split down the center, assumingly from the weight of the tree when it fell. The tree had just missed the structure by feet. From this distance, he could see the finer details of the cabin. The builder had used wood planks for the siding, and while most were still intact, large sections had rotted out, leaving fist-sized holes randomly dispersed all around. At least one window had been shattered. Ethan couldn't imagine anyone staying there. The difficulty of keeping the place warm with all the drafts would be challenging enough. The risk of the structure caving in from the bowed walls and sagging roof made it a risk hardly worth taking.

Ethan decided to continue around to the back of the cabin. Behind it, he found a door and another window, which had been shattered out at some point. This one had been covered with a blanket, that looked in much better condition than he had expected one to look had it been there for years.

Ethan walked up to the blanket-covered window, pulled the sheet to the side, and climbed through; confident no one was inside. To his disbelief, the wood floors were sturdy. At least the portion he found himself on. Ethan grabbed his flashlight, flipping it on to fill the darkness. The room he had entered looked to be a kitchen. There were no modern appliances, so he suspected the house had been abandoned long before they became common. Or the previous occupants simply decided to forego them. There were paper plates on a wooden table against the far wall, he could tell they had recently been brought in. His heartbeat echoed from the walls as a new kind of cold entered his blood.

Ethan turned his light in the opposite direction to a doorway. He followed his beam toward it, testing each step before committing to it. Once he passed through the doorway, he found himself in what felt like a living room. The shattered window, as well as the two long rotted boards of siding, had been stuffed with rags or blankets. Directly to the left of the door was a table with sheets of something on top. Ethan turned his focus to the table, taking the pages into his hand before realizing they were photos.

The photos were of the shack burning, taken from no more than 100 yards. Ethan struggled to tell the true distance because the darkness around the flames offered no depth perception. He also wasn't sure if they had been taken with some sort of telescoping lens. Half a dozen photos of the house burning, one with a shadowed figure watching, stood between the photographer and the house.

Ethan wondered if there were pictures of Vargas's murder, too. It was something he would have loved to see, but also the idea of it sent a surge of fear through him. The photographer had been there when the shack had been torched and when Vargas had been murdered. They were likely involved, but they were also following him. They could get close to these situations without detection. Ethan might never see them coming. They were on a mission to clean up a mess, leaving no piece left behind.

Ethan returned the photos in the same orientation he thought he had picked them up from. He began quietly calling out for John, unsure if he was speaking loud enough for his voice to carry more than a few feet. He kicked the floor once, which sounded solid. There was relief knowing he wouldn't have to check a basement. It didn't look like the cabin had more than one floor, either, so he continued through the main level methodically. Ethan tested each step, careful not to put too much weight anywhere that protested, even slightly.

The house had been a giant square, wrapping back to the kitchen he had first entered. There had been a ladder leading to an upper area, but he abandoned it after hearing nothing when he called out to John. The idea of going up there caused instant vertigo, forcing him to grab a wall just to stay standing.

Ethan stood in the kitchen once he completed the squared lap. He began debating with himself whether to explore more or leave. His decision was made for him when he heard the roaring of a small motor, which he guessed to be an ATV. Ethan spun to the window, climbing through it. As he fell into the snow under the window, he heard the fabric of the sheet tear.

He ran to the wood line, ducking behind a log as a flood of lights entered the house. It looked like LED lanterns, but he couldn't be sure. From his position and with the light cascading across the sheet covering the window, he could tell he shredded the left side. He knew he had made a mess of the snow outside, too. There was nothing he could do about it, other than hope they wouldn't notice. But they might notice the wet footprints throughout the house. Ethan hoped by that time, they would assume they had made the tracks.

Ethan kept low as he rounded the house, sticking close to the trees. He saw two men standing inside, visible through the missing front door. He wasn't sure how many others might be in there, if any, but the two seemed to be talking. He was sure neither was John.

Ethan would go home and call Klein. He could tell him about the people shacking up in the dilapidated cabin and the pictures of the fire. That would incentivize him to investigate and hopefully, if they did have John, get him out of there safely—a lot more safely than if he went in there starting a gunfight with a bolt-action rifle.

Chapter 33

Once inside the cabin, he watched out of the front window for a while, waiting to see if anyone had followed him back. When his breath had fogged the window, blocking any visibility, he pulled himself away. He started the fire in the stove and settled down in a chair directly in the center of the living area. He would sit there all night, in the one place in the entire cabin that provided him direct view of the front and both sides of the house. If anyone came onto his property from either of those three directions, he would know. Ethan left the television off and the front latch to the stove closed, leaving himself in near complete darkness. He would be able to see them from the moon's reflecting light bouncing from the snow, but they would only see darkness. He hoped, if they approached at all, it would be from the front of the house. Ethan knew if they did that, he would get at least two clean shots off before they found any sort of cover.

Ethan leaned back in the chair, finding a comfortable position for the long night; one he could adjust to and shoulder his rifle if needed. As he watched the growing wind blow the white mounds outside, his thoughts drifted to the last conversation he had with Vargas.

Ethan walked into the private conference room of the prison shortly after noon. He didn't know what the meeting was about other than Vargas had asked to see him. He knew Vargas had a history of blackmailing or, in some way, threatening past DAs. It was how he had beaten a lot of his previous charges. But it was something Ethan wasn't worried about. He lived in a gated community, had close ties to several high-ranking officers, and had a pristine record he honored deeply. He was untouchable.

Only a few minutes after Ethan had pulled the files from his briefcase, arranging them in an orderly fashion so he could find whatever he might need during the meeting, the steel door opened with a rattling clank. Vargas entered with his feet shackled and his hands cuffed in front of his body. Two correctional officers had their arms interwoven with his on either side. Vargas waddled under their control to an empty seat across from Ethan. The guards plopped him down. One bent over, connecting a new set of restraints to the shackles on his feet before connecting them to a U-bolt permanently inserted into the concrete floor.

Vargas's eyes never left Ethan's.

"You have twenty minutes," the standing guard said before he and his partner left. The metal door slammed behind them.

"Is your attorney on their way?" Ethan asked as a matter of covering his bases.

"Come on, amigo, we don't need anyone else here."

"As a matter of fact, we do. I cannot speak with you without your representation here."

"I called you here because I wanted to talk to you, hermano. If I wanted them here, I would've asked for them. No?"

Ethan let out a sigh, releasing the frustration from realizing he had wasted half his afternoon driving down to the prison for no reason. He grabbed the files in one hand, forcing the briefcase open with the other. "We have nothing to discuss. Next time you waste my time, I'll add intimidation to your charges." Ethan stood forcefully, walking straight toward the door.

"Don't get wound up, counselor. I want to make a deal."

Ethan stopped. He had wanted to make a deal with Vargas the day he was arrested. A man in his position could turn the table on a lot of people. It would allow Ethan to leap several rungs on his career ladder. A case like this would boost his political aspirations. "Then call your attorney and schedule a new meeting."

"I bet your esposa Kristina and beautiful hija Mary would be very sad if something were to happen to you on the way home, hermano. Was she named after the Holy Mother?"

Ethan's blood felt as though it had stopped moving, pooling inside of him instead. His head pounded with his grip tightening around the handle of his briefcase. With Vargas sitting there, chained to the floor, he was defenseless. Still, Ethan knew he could take one swing with his briefcase and put the maggot out of his misery. Save everyone time and energy, not to mention cost. But then he would have to explain his actions to the world. Unlike Vargas, he had a conscience, and guilt welled up behind the throbbing in his head as the thought passed, his grip relaxing.

Ethan rounded the table again, reclaiming his spot across from Vargas.

"Good, hermano. I'm glad we talk like men and not have to resort to such ugly tactics."

"I'm not your brother, Mr. Vargas. You're a criminal who is about to spend the rest of your life locked behind a cage. What makes you think that'll change?"

"I think there's a way we can both win," Vargas's lips tilted into a slimy grin.

"If you reveal everything about your operation and every other operation you have intel on, I will consider letting you keep your life."

Vargas laughed mockingly. "I'll keep my life either way. I had a different arrangement in mind."

"What's that?" Ethan gripped his pen in his right hand, willing the building tension to leave his body and go anywhere else.

"I won't betray anyone; you get me ten years in a medium-security prison. That way, I'm out in five, and I can keep my men fed."

Ethan tried to return a mocking laugh, but he heard the anxiety in it. "Why would I let you only do five years for everything you're being charged with? What do we get out of the deal?"

"I will let you see your family again, para uno. I will also personally guarantee neither I nor anyone in my organización will transport through your city again. Think about it, hermano, you'd be a hero. The man who scared away the big bad wolf."

"Putting you away for life would do the same thing."

"Oh, no, Señor Barret. It might help for a while, but others would take my place. If I'm out there, I can protect your city." Vargas leaned closer, crossing his fingers together as his brown eyes pierced Ethan's. "I hear it from people I trust very much. You and your wife are having a rough time. Paying for a divorce and putting a young girl through school can be very expensive, no? I can give you five million dollars for your agreement to my terms. That can do a lot of good for you and your familia. Besides, everyone will forget I only got five in a year or two. I'll be old news by then, pareja."

Ethan's eyes wandered up to the camera in the corner. He suspected it was off because he assumed the guards, like him, thought Vargas's attorney would be in the room. Protecting him from being recorded. But he wasn't positive. Saying the wrong thing could get him in a position he could never escape, and for what? The promises made by a murdering drug lord? Ethan grabbed a blank sheet of paper from his briefcase.

Ethan knew if he could make it seem as though he was the one to keep the threat of Angel Vargas off the streets, he would be able to go from the DA's office straight to mayorship. Kristina would appreciate the fact all of his hard work had paid off and it would give him more time to save the marriage. He spent a great deal of time around politicians, and he knew his work schedule as the district attorney was at least double theirs. Taking the deal with Vargas, as vile as it made him feel, solved a lot of problems. He could hide his tracks well enough to keep the spotlight off of him, even if Vargas went against his word and reported Ethan. There were ways to hide the money trail. There were ways to make sure his actions appeared just and in the best interest of his office. It was a risk worth taking.

"That is the most ridiculous thing I've ever heard," he said as he wrote on the page. "This is my counteroffer. You can take it or leave it." He spun the page around, sliding it in front of Vargas.

Vargas read the agreement; *Yes*.

"Si, señor. I think that is fair."

"Good," Ethan said, grabbing the paper and stuffing it back into his briefcase. "I will write up the plea bargain and get it over to your attorney by the end of the day."

"You're a fair man, Señor Barret. I won't forget your kindness."

"It's not for you. It's for my family and my city. If it were up to me, you'd rot under this prison."

Vargas lowered his voice to an almost inaudible whisper. "Make sure you stick to your end of it. It's hard for a man to watch everything he loves burn to the ground, which is exactly what'll happen if you don't see this through."

Ethan stepped closer to Vargas than he cared to—had it not been for the chains holding him at bay he wouldn't have taken it. He lowered his voice as he spoke. "If you come near my family, or threaten them again, I will make sure you rot in your cell. I will make it my personal mission to destroy you and your entire organization."

A condescending smile wrapped Vargas's face. "You got more fight than you look like." He leaned back in his chair, turning his head more toward Ethan. "But you'd be wise to not make promises you can't keep."

Ethan's fingers gripped the rawhide handles of his briefcase tighter. He could feel the leather spreading as his fingernails dug into it. A brief flash of him swinging the hard-covered case down over Vargas's head startled him. Ethan turned, buzzing the guard before the small voice in the back of his mind won.

❦

Sitting in the darkness of his cabin, accepting his life now for what it was, he wished he had hit Vargas. Surely, he could've gotten a reduced sentence. If nothing else, his family may be alive. They could be living the life they should've had, regardless of what had happened to him. Instead, he swallowed the anger like he always did and walked away. The judge threw the plea out and his family paid the price for his choice to make a deal with the devil. All of it could've been avoided if he had only been a little stronger.

He didn't know who had killed Vargas. He didn't care, either. Ethan wanted to shake their hand, thanking them for giving him the justice he knew he'd never see otherwise. Then, the rational thought came, the person who killed Vargas and torched the shack was probably the same person who'd been targeting him. It was probably the same person who might've taken John. It may have even been the person behind his own torture that had unfolded in the past year. Killing Vargas may have been nothing more than tying up a loose end, which meant Ethan was the last fray in the line.

Chapter 34

Ethan woke to the sun hitting his face from the east window, overlooking the side of his property. The sun was pushing above the tree line, which meant he had slept until after 7:30 a.m. He wasn't sure when he had fallen asleep, but he cursed himself for letting himself become vulnerable through the night.

He heard crunching from outside, firing his brain into full alert. He bounced up from his chair, swinging his rifle toward the front window and lining his sights up to where he heard the growing sound of churning gravel. He let out a relieved sigh at the sight of Detective Klein's unmarked car, despite knowing his presence meant nothing good for him. He could at least tell him what he saw the night before. Ethan's pride, which drove the desire to keep his situation under wraps, had faded through the night. He knew he was in over his head. Now, with John missing, not knowing where he might be or even if he were alive, he knew he needed more help than a long-ago-retired army vet and himself.

Ethan slid his feet into his untied boots, opening the door as his left heel hit the bottom of the shoe. He ventured outside, resting his rifle on the porch before Klein could take him for a threat.

"I'm glad to see you," Ethan said, clearing the steps of the porch in two strides. "I was going to call you today."

"We'll see how excited you are to see me after we talk."

Dread forced itself into Ethan's body. "Why is that?"

Klein raised a plastic baggie Ethan hadn't noticed he was holding. "You dropped something." Inside the bag was a gold chain. One he recognized right away. It was the one he had given Kristina on their first anniversary. Unconsciously, he slid his hand into his pocket, finding it empty. "We traced it back to you. I can't help but wonder what it was doing on my crime scene."

Ethan backed up to the porch, sitting on the second step putting him closer to his rifle. Out of instinct, Klein's hand found the butt of his pistol. "I haven't been frank with you," Ethan sighed. "I was out there before the fire."

"Why? Were you a customer?" Klein put the baggy into his pocket, approaching Ethan with caution. He kept a safe distance in case Ethan lunged, but he wanted to be close enough that Ethan would feel supported. It helped suspects open more in conversation if they felt a sense of closeness from the investigator.

Ethan shook his head. "Someone has been coming onto my property. At first, I thought it was just a poacher or trespasser. Then I realized they were stalking me. Naturally, I thought it was

Vargas. I had heard those guys over the ridge were in the drug trade, so I thought maybe they worked for him. Somehow, he found out I was here, too." Ethan took a deep breath, unable to comprehend how his life brought him to this moment. "My friend and I went over there just to see if we could spot Vargas. You know, to confirm he was here, so we could call the police. But things spiraled. They were attacked, Vargas ended up dead, and now my friend is missing. I don't know what the hell is happening."

Klein nodded as if he understood the predicament Ethan found himself in. "Why didn't you call us the second you suspected Vargas had found you?"

Ethan gave him a serious glare. "Your department isn't equipped to deal with the likes of Vargas."

Klein nodded again. "What difference does it make whether you called us when you simply suspected he was out here versus confirming it?"

"If I knew he was out here, I would feel more prepared. If I didn't, I would just have a bunch of cops and feds trampling through my life for nothing."

"Maybe. But I think there's more. I think you didn't want us to know he was out here because then you could deal out some vigilante justice. I think you spotted him there that day and went back later. You poured the gas on the back of the house and set it on fire, then when Vargas came out, you executed him. Maybe your friend started feeling some kind of way about it. So you put a bullet in his head, too."

"I can prove I had nothing to do with it," Ethan argued.

"How?"

"There's a cabin a couple of miles down this road," he pointed to his left. "I went out there last night thinking whoever took John may have been holding him there. I didn't see anyone when I got there, so I went inside. I found pictures of the shack being burned down. I barely got out of it before two guys came back. They're probably part of the crew that took out Vargas."

"A crew? We didn't see anything that suggested more than one or two people were involved."

"Call for a unit to meet you there. I'm telling you; you'll find them there."

"I'll tell you what, I'll entertain your story by taking *you* down there. I'll search the cabin, but if there's no one there, you come down to the station and talk to me there."

"Fine," Ethan said, standing from the stoop. He grabbed his rifle.

"Leave it here."

"I'm not going out there unarmed."

"Yes, you are."

Ethan's eyes protested, but he could tell it was a losing battle. He opened the door enough to slip the rifle through, then locked the door.

Ethan's stomach trembled the entire drive down the crumbling road. As the sun continued to rise, the snow began to melt more, causing the dirt beneath it to grow soggy. Klein's tires struggled in spots to grab real estate, spinning unserviceably before gripping something and moving the SUV forward in a jerking motion. At the base of the drive leading to the cabin, a fallen tree prevented them from going any further, something Ethan hadn't noticed in the darkness of the night before. The ATV tracks could be seen passing the far left of the log between another tree. It was far too narrow for the vehicle they were in to pass. But Ethan pointed it out, anyway.

"Those are the tracks from the ATVs they were on last night."

"Those could be from anyone. Kids wanting to take advantage of the snow."

"In the middle of the night?"

"Kids do dumber things. You stay here, I'll check out the cabin."

Ethan unbuckled his belt. "I'm going with you. I want to make sure you actually go inside."

"Yes, Mr. Barret, I drove us down here just to pretend to go into the structure."

"I'm a former DA. No offense, but I know better than to just take the police's word on their investigative tactics."

Klein's eyes narrowed as if the words had been the sourest thing he had ever encountered. "With respect, the key phrase there is *former*. You no longer have any right to be involved in any investigation. Not to mention, you're a primary suspect in this particular one."

"I get that. But I am also, currently, a free man. This is abandoned property that is not officially related to any known crime. I have every right to be in there."

Klein groaned as he climbed out of the SUV. Ethan followed suit, hoping the two men he had spotted the night before had John inside. Ethan waited for Klein to lead the way, but he noticed the detective leaning back into his vehicle. He reappeared with an AR-15, pulling the strap over his shoulder as he chambered a round.

"I thought you were sure I was lying?"

"In case you're not, I'd like to be prepared. Now, stay behind me. You can go up to the cabin, but you stay outside. I don't need you falling through any flooring or bumping into a post that sends the whole thing crumbling down."

Ethan nodded, knowing fully he would be going inside. He didn't trust Klein any more than Klein trusted him.

Chapter 35

In the light of day, the cabin was in more disrepair than Ethan had realized. The bowing walls and sinking roof seemed twice as bad as they had the night before. The gaping holes scattered throughout the siding were large enough for a person to walk through in some places. The house, he realized, likely served as a darkroom for them to develop their film. But it wasn't a place they would likely hole up in. Certainly, not a place they would keep a hostage. Too much risk of the whole structure folding in on itself to be a viable location.

Klein called out to the vast wilderness and the cabin which created an ugliness within it, ordering anyone in the area to step outside. There was no response, as Ethan expected since the two ATVs were not parked outside where they had been the night before. He didn't know when they had left, but it hadn't been since he and Klein had arrived. The engines disrupted the silence of the woods, making a quiet getaway impossible. But there was a silver lining in that. They could explore the house in the light of day, making navigating the treacherous structure easier. Ethan knew he could've missed a door when he had been in there the previous night. Now, it would be easier to find if John was inside somewhere.

"They're gone," Ethan told him after Klein shouted his orders for the second time.

"How do you know that?" Klein shifted his eyes to look in Ethan's direction; his stance and face were unchanged.

"Their ATVs are gone."

Klein relaxed his stance, lowering his rifle enough to approach the house without risking a fall. He reached the blanket-covered entrance and used the barrel of his rifle to move it away, peeking around it to get a glance inside the cabin. Once sure nothing was inside waiting to ambush him—human or animal—he shifted his body slightly to face Ethan. "Stay here."

Ethan nodded but waited only long enough for Klein to disappear behind the blanket, which fell like a closing curtain before he followed him in. Klein was moving down the side hallway by the time Ethan entered the structure. He stood by what should've been the front door, trying to remember his path of travel last night. To his right, he saw the kitchen, which he thought was where he had entered the house. The window he thought he had come in from was within his eyesight, which meant the table with the photos should be within his reach from where he stood now. Except the only table he saw was bare, revealing nothing more than rotting spots around the corners.

Ethan headed toward the hall Klein had gone in, hoping he was simply wrong about the room he had been in. He knew the hall would lead around the house in a square path, ending up right where he started. As he went room to room, everything was gone. There were no pictures, no cots, nothing that had been there the night before was there now. Ethan was filled with dread, realizing he must've not put something back exactly right. They must've noticed, got spooked, and left the cabin.

Ethan ended up back in the main room where he had started. Klein stood relaxed by the frame of the front door, gingerly leaning his shoulder against it with the rifle hanging from his shoulder. His arms were crossed over his chest as if to say *told you so.*

"They were here, dammit!" Ethan shouted.

"Well, no one is here now." Klein straightened his body, "I indulged you on this. Now, I need you to come to the station and have a chat with me."

"They might still be close by. We can follow the ATV tracks to wherever they went."

Klein's tone grew stern, "I'm not wandering through the woods on a wild goose chase. I told you kids could've made those tracks. Now, either you can come with me compliantly, or I can arrest you. Either way, you will be coming down to the station."

Ethan shook his head, defeated. "Unless you plan on driving me back, I need to get my truck." Ethan knew John's car would be easier, but he didn't know where he had put the key. For all he knew, they were on John. A part of him also hoped the truck would get caught in the mud behind the house, buying him a little more time to figure out answers to the questions he knew Klein would ask.

He had no one to corroborate his story or his whereabouts, and he knew everything pointed at him. If Ethan had been sitting across the table from someone else in the same position, he would've felt confident he could get a conviction on the circumstantial evidence available.

❦

Stepping into the police station was a strange type of alternate reality. It had been something he had done hundreds of times in his previous life, but this was a different station and this time he was being escorted by police as a suspect. Not as an ally ready to break down the suspect and their defense attorney.

The station, though entirely different from the one in Indianapolis, was the same. A reception area staged with chairs, a long glass window opposite the front door with several windows for numerous needs. A wooden door to the side of the windows provided entry to the main part of the station. Doors lined the hall. Most holding interrogation rooms, but some, Ethan suspected, were offices of high-ranking members of the force. Beyond the hall would be the squad room where the departments would intermingle. Ethan guessed the main difference between here and Indianapolis was that detectives would work everything that came their way. There probably weren't specialties. He doubted they had a bunk room for detectives to catch up on rest or a weight room. As similar as it was, it was very different.

Klein put a hand on Ethan's shoulder near the end of the hall to stop him. Klein opened a door to Ethan's right. The detective's arm extended into the small room. "Have a seat and I'll be right back. Do you want anything to drink?"

Ethan shook his head as he walked into the room. The small-eight foot by eight-foot room was designed for discomfort. The overhead lights were too bright, making the once-white paint sting his eyes. There was a small metal table attached to the wall and a matching metal bench on either side, which he knew would be uncomfortable and cold. Everything in there was designed to make the suspect feel uneasy. It would force them to say anything to get out of there. He knew Klein would be in another room watching the video feed, looking for a tell. Klein would be looking for something he could use to get Ethan to admit to the things Ethan knew he was innocent of. Ethan turned to find the small CCTV camera in the corner of the room, situated for a perfect view of the table.

Ethan took a deep breath. The guilty were often more nervous than the innocent. He wasn't nervous as much as frustrated. Still, he didn't want to give Klein any emotions that could be used as ammunition. Ethan slowed his mind, allowing it to go as blank as possible. He wanted to hear the questions in their entirety, to catch the nuances designed to trip a suspect into saying something that implied guilt. Ethan himself had gotten confessions from people who were later proved innocent; he knew how easily it could happen. If he let his frustration get the better of him, he could fall into the same traps. Ethan took one more deep breath before going to the cold steel seat.

Only a few minutes passed before Klein returned with a yellow legal pad in one hand and a frosted Coke can in the other. He sat across from Ethan, setting the pad down before popping the tab of his drink. He took a long, hard swig, making his pleasure audible when the can parted from his lips. "Man, that's good. Are you sure you don't want anything? We have Cokes, pizza, probably some baked stuff."

Ethan smiled politely. He was fully aware Klein was trying to make it feel informal. It was just another conversation with little weight so that Ethan would let his guard down. If he took anything to drink, they would keep it for DNA, which they could find anyway if they went through the effort. He had done an ancestry kit years ago and donated blood in the past. "I'm fine. I would just like to answer your questions so I can get back home before anyone notices I'm not there."

"Who might notice that?"

"The same people who were stalking me, that killed Vargas and those guys, and took my friend." Ethan created space between him and Klein, showing he wasn't falling for the chummy act. "The one you refuse to look for."

"You have to admit, it all sounds pretty far-fetched. Why would anyone be that interested in you? Unless there's more you haven't told me."

"I was the DA. I put a lot of people behind bars, including a detective. And they all had associates, family, and friends. Even if it wasn't Vargas that was targeting me, I'm sure we had a lot of the same enemies."

"I'm glad you bring the DA thing up. For someone with your track record, I find it peculiar you'd go so far out of your way to not get the police involved. Especially if you feel a man like Vargas has tracked you down and kidnapped your friend."

Ethan slammed his fist down on the cold steel of the tabletop. He took a moment to compose himself after giving Klein the first bit of ammunition he'd been looking for. "I told you yesterday that he was missing. You didn't do anything about it when you could have. That falls on you."

"You seem to have a hot streak, Ethan. Has that ever turned violent?"

"Never," Ethan told him.

"What about when you attacked Manuel Rodrigez in front of an entire department?" A smug smile sat on Klein's face.

"Extreme emotional distress," Ethan told him. "I had just found out Angel Vargas killed my family. I knew Rodrigez was a close associate of his. When I saw him coming into the station, I snapped."

"Maybe you snapped the same way when you saw Vargas?" Judgement flickered in his eyes.

Ethan shook his head adamantly. "There's a big difference between a fifteen-second fight and setting a whole house on fire, kneeling a man down, shooting him in the head, and burying him."

"Is there? I could understand why you'd want Vargas dead. I really can. Hell, if I were in your shoes, I would've done much worse."

"Is there something you'd like to admit, detective?"

Klein smiled. "I'm just saying, if you did kill him, no one here would blame you. You'd probably be crowned a hero by most of them."

"I hope you're sure to tell that to whoever did it when you find them."

"Let's pretend someone else tracked him down and did everything over there. I still don't understand why they'd be so interested in you that they'd stalk you or take your friend. Especially if you haven't heard from them? Who takes a person and doesn't ask for a ransom or something else in return?"

Ethan hadn't considered that. Although, he wasn't easy to contact. He had made sure of that. "Maybe when he was alone in the cabin, they took him because I wasn't there. It was more about opportunity than intent. I can't speak as to why they haven't reached out for anything."

Then Ethan remembered his confession to John. The five million dollar buy-off Vargas had given him. John was the only person that knew about it. There hadn't been any sign of John trying to fight whoever had taken him. Ethan brought his hands under the table, squeezing them tightly together to conceal the fumes building in him. Maybe he had been right to not trust John.

"Maybe. But there's a lot of land out there. Maybe he wanted to go to the police about what you two did and you couldn't have that. Maybe you killed him and buried him out there. I did see you coming back with a gun in the middle of a snowstorm. I've never been the best hunter myself, but I know enough that it's not a time most people go out."

"I'm trying to be self-sufficient. I don't have the luxury of waiting for perfect weather."

"Maybe." Klein wrote something in his notepad.

"I've answered all the questions I'm going to answer. If you have any more questions, give me a call so I can have my attorney meet me here."

"We're just having a friendly chat, Ethan. Stay a while longer. I don't have many more questions."

"I've answered everything I can. I've told you all I know. I'll get you my lawyer's number, and you can call him with any other questions."

"You're a smart man, you know the game. Bringing a lawyer into it only makes you look more guilty."

"And you're too smart to think I'd buy that line of crap. It's obvious you have no intention of helping me find my friend. I will be trying to save him before they do to him what they did to Vargas, while you keep digging down an empty rabbit hole."

Klein nodded. "Very convincing, Mr. Barret." Klein stood from his place on the bench. "I can't have an innocent casualty on my conscience. I'll put out an APB for your friend. I will include all ATVs on it as well. If you hear from anyone about a ransom, I expect you to call me the second it happens. Otherwise, I can't help but think you're somehow linked to it." Klein stuck his hand out for Ethan to take.

He did, shaking it. "I'll keep you in the loop. I just hope I don't have to bury anyone else I care about because you were too narrow-sighted to look past me."

"I hope so, too."

Chapter 36

Ethan returned home by mid-afternoon. He parked the truck in his usual spot, no longer concerned if anyone knew he was there or not. Whatever edge he hoped hiding the truck would provide had vanished days ago. He exited the truck, his eyes glued to the gravel before him. His mind raced in different directions, seemingly without purpose. He had spent the entire drive back home replaying the interrogation in his mind, then trailing off to hoping he could figure out a plan to track down John. Neither scenario he played in his mind provided him with any promise. Ethan assumed Klein would put a detail on him, limiting how much he could do in trying to track down the men he saw at the cabin. Of course, now that temperatures hovered in the mid-fifties, most of the snow had melted. Any tracks they might have left for him to follow would be gone.

As far as he could tell from the interrogation, he had lost his temper, unable to contain himself as much as he had hoped. But he knew he was innocent of the accusations; he had given viable options for Klein to track down other than himself. Ethan only hoped the detective would keep his word on taking John's disappearance more seriously.

Ethan reached his door, his keys already in hand. As he slid the key into the lock, his senses sent a signal, forcing him to pause. He looked up to see a sheet of paper fastened to the door by a pocket knife, a generic one found at any second-hand shop. Still, after he ripped the page free from the blade, he put the edge between his lips. Ethan tucked his hand into his sleeve to pull the knife free. With his hands covered, he closed the blade into the handle and opened the door. He set the knife on the counter, making a mental note to put it into a baggie. But first, he pulled the page from his lips to read the pasted-on letters clipped from the pages of some magazine.

It's time to collect.

Ethan crumbled up the sheet, tossing it back toward the wood stove. If it was the money they were coming to collect, they could have it. He didn't want it anymore. It was the source of all his torment. He wished he had never taken it, to begin with.

Ethan went back outside, descended the steps, and went under the porch. Near his log pile, he grabbed his shovel. Ethan headed back around the right side of the house toward the rear. He dropped to his knees, entering the crawl space beneath his cabin. He crawled ten shovel lengths forward, then three lengths to his left, ending near the center of the house. Space was a premium, but he had made the dig once. He could do it again. Ethan shoved the rock marking his burial spot to the side, then began digging a shallow hole with his hands. The shovel was more a way to measure his crawling than to dig up the duffle bag he had wrapped in plastic and buried nine months ago.

Due to the constraints in space, he hadn't dug deep the first time. Which he was thankful for. He felt the plastic of the bag just as his hand was beginning to cramp. He focused more on the edges of the bag until he could pull it free from the hole. Once he had his arm wrapped around it, he began crawling backward toward the opening of the crawl space, pulling the bag with him as he moved.

Once he felt the air of the outside world, he propped himself up on his knees, keeping the bag under the house. He looked around, ensuring no one was there to ambush him. Either Klein or whoever was coming to *collect*. When he felt confident no one was there waiting for him to come out, he reached back under the house to retrieve the bag. He forced himself up, tucking the bag under his arm as he walked briskly back to the porch, barging into his house and locking the door behind him.

He suddenly felt very alone. It was a somber realization that made his skin grow cold. There was no guarantee that they wouldn't kill him once they got the money. He wondered if the note had been their way of asking for a ransom because, as he thought about it, they had made no mention of John. Ethan felt a rising sense of confidence in his suspicion that John hadn't been taken at all. He willingly left, and he was the one asking for the money.

Ethan cut the plastic from the duffle bag, sliding it free. He pulled the zipper, revealing three bundles of cash, equaling approximately $1.5 million, if he remembered correctly. He had put another $1.5 million in an off-shore account—the account and routing number were somewhere in the bag. Ethan would have to go to the other side of the property for the rest of the money. He had known keeping it all in one location would prove catastrophic, except now that he was prepared to be rid of it, separating the cash was becoming more of a liability than he expected.

Ethan closed the bag again, taking it back to his room. He opened his closet, sliding the heavy bag to the back, stacking a box and unwashed clothing over it.

Ethan made his way back to the living area, where he found his phone sitting on the counter. He turned it on, partially surprised to see there was still battery life since he couldn't recall the last time he had charged the thing. He tapped the phone icon and dialed a number he pulled from memory.

The phone rang twice before a petite voice answered, "Lang Investigations. How may I direct your call?"

"Marshall Lang, please. This is Ethan Barret." Marshall Lang had been the one and only private investigator Ethan rode along with during an investigation. He was a visible force with a shaved head because he felt it was easier to disguise himself if an investigation called for it. Ethan wasn't sure what the man's natural hair color was, if he truly needed glasses, or if they had simply become part of his ever-changing appearance. But he was good at what he did, always getting results. More importantly to Ethan, he knew Mason Sharp, the investigator John often used and was supposed to call for a background check on Beaver.

"Ethan. I didn't think I'd hear from you today, of all days," his deep voice had a smoothness to it that radiated.

Ethan pulled the phone from his ear to check the date. He had intentionally not checked the date each day and made it a point to stay busy. He hoped he wouldn't know when the anniversary had come. He hoped he would've worked through it and at some point realize it had passed. Instead, he was there on November 2nd, forced to know it had been one years since his family was murdered.

"Are you calling about your case? Because I don't have anything for you. I wish to hell I did."

"No," Ethan stammered, swallowing his shame. "I'm calling to see if you've spoken to Mason Sharp recently."

"No, can't say that I have. It's been a few days. He said he was working something big, something that was going to finally let him retire. Lucky bastard, my body's taken a beating over the years. A cold beer and a hot beach is exactly what I need."

"You say he's been gone a few days? Did he say where he was going?"

"No. Just that he got a big lead and was following up. When he got back, he'd be putting in his retirement notice and closing up shop." There was a brief pause. "What's this about? Is everything okay?"

"I think so. I just had something I wanted to run by him, but if he's about to hit the big time, he doesn't have time for me."

"I'd be happy to help you out. What were you needing?"

"Nothing serious. You know, I save you for the most important stuff."

Another pause. "So, are you back practicing law? I hadn't heard anything about it."

"No—I—I just wanted a background run on someone I was thinking of hiring for a remodel project out here. But it's not that important."

"Okay, well it was great hearing from you. And my thoughts are with you today."

"Thank you, Marshall. I appreciate that."

Ethan ended the call, checking the time before he sat the phone back down. It was 4 p.m., which meant he had a couple hours before nightfall. He suspected if John and Mason hadn't shown up by now, they were waiting for the concealment of night. He had time to get one more thing out of the way before they came to collect the money. He knew whether he gave it away willingly or not, the night would end with him dead. Ethan knew he should've trusted that nagging sense that he should've sent John away. But John had been his best friend—his only friend—which he thought meant something.

Chapter 37

Ethan stepped out of his truck in the center of Beaver's driveway. He saw Beaver rocking on his porch, a fat cigar between his parted lips, a steaming cup of something in his hand.

"Wasn't expectin' to see you this evening. Cigar?"

Ethan waived off the offer, leaning against the porch railing opposite Beaver.

"I just wanted to thank you for all your help. I wouldn't have survived the last year without it."

Beaver's brow raised questioningly. "Well, anytime you need somethin', you know where I am."

"I know." Ethan had searched for the right words to say to Beaver, but the short drive hadn't provided the opportunity to discover them as he'd hoped. "I don't want to alarm you, but I wouldn't feel right if I said nothing. No matter what you hear tonight, stay home."

Beaver pulled the cigar from his lips, slowing his pace in the rocker. "What might I hear? Just so I know if it's somethin' I should be checkin' in on or not."

"No matter what you hear, I want you to stay home. I don't want you getting yourself caught up in my mess."

Beaver shrugged. "If I hear somethin' concerning, I can't promise I won't go checkin' on it. I gotta protect my land. And my neighbors."

"The best thing you can do to help me is to stay home. It'll all make sense tomorrow."

"Okay," Beaver huffed. "I guess I can do that. What kind of shit you get yourself into, boy?"

"Do you remember when you told me there's a lot of reasons a man buries his past?"

Beaver's eyes said he did.

"Turns out I didn't bury mine deep enough. It's come back on me."

"This got somethin' to do with your family?" Beaver took a hit from his cigar before tossing it over the rail into the yard.

Ethan nodded. "I went against everything I stood for to make a deal with an evil man. I took his blood money, and when he felt I went against our deal, he killed my family. Some of my former colleagues found out, so they're going to take the money off my hands."

"And you're suspectin' you'll put up a fight for it?"

Ethan lowered his eyes, shaking his head. "They can have the money. I just have a feeling there's only one way things can end tonight. Whether I'm right or wrong, I don't want you getting caught up in the mix. I already got you too involved. You've done more than I should've ever asked of you."

"You know, good neighbors are hard to come by. I ain't too fond of the idea of havin' to find a new one."

"I'll leave the deed under my mattress, signed over to you. No one has to know whether you paid for it or not. Then you don't have to worry about any neighbors."

Beaver stood from his rocker, extending his hand for Ethan. "It was a pleasure knowin' you, Ethan."

"You too, Beaver."

"You know, finding a new neighbor is one thing. But finding a new friend is much harder. I don't have many friends left these days, and I'd like to think you're one of them."

Ethan offered one last smile to Beaver, returning the sentiment, before making his way back to his truck. He had half an hour of daylight left.

When he got back to the cabin, he drove the truck to the far end of his property near the dead maple tree. He had buried the second bag on the side of the tree facing the house. It was much easier to retrieve than the first, despite the mud, because he could use the shovel instead of his hands. Once he saw the top of the trash bag covering the duffle inside, he wrapped his hands around it. He tossed it into the back of the truck and went to the cabin just as darkness claimed the last bit of the day.

Chapter 38

Ethan paced around the cabin's living area for nearly ninety minutes before the gentle hum of the ATV motors broke the silence outside. They were coming from the rear of his property, growing louder with each passing second. They stopped somewhere behind the cabin. He went to the counter, tucking the revolver into his front waistband and hoisting the duffle bags onto his shoulders. He went out to the front porch, cautiously descending the steps, making sure he didn't fall. Once he rounded the house, he spotted the two ATVs, easily recognizable from the dilapidated cabin he had gone into. He expected to see John waiting. At the very least, approaching the front of the house from the ATVs, but he wasn't there.

Ethan dropped the bags into the wet grass, calling out to John.

He wasn't surprised when John came from the back of the cabin, trailed by Mason Sharp. Mason had lost a bit of weight since Ethan had last seen him, but his thick glasses still hung from the bridge of his nose. A black skullcap hugged his balding hairline.

"I should've known you were involved when you left the pictures," Ethan said to Mason. "And I should've trusted my instincts with you," he told John.

"A lot of things should've gone differently, Ethan. But they didn't, so we find ourselves here." John's face was partially hidden in the darkness, but there was something different about him.

"An interesting time to extort me," Ethan declared, looking down at the bags resting on either side of him. "The night of the anniversary."

"I think it's the perfect night," Mason countered.

"What better night than the night you killed the woman I loved?"

Ethan's throat locked on him. Of the many different responses he had and hadn't expected, that response made no sense to him. Finally, he found his voice. "What?"

"Don't play stupid, Ethan. It's just us out here. You might've fooled the cops, but you're not fooling us. This was never about the damn money. It's always been about her," John's voice was almost a growl.

"And we have proof you did it," Mason added. "As you've seen."

"Who are you talking about? Who was the love of your life? Who the hell do you think I killed?"

"Stop playing games!" John screamed as he barged toward John from the shadows. His face contorted in an angry flash. "You found the letters. You knew Kristina was going to leave you for me. That's why you killed her!"

It was as if an ice pick entered Ethan's chest, sending cold through his veins and causing a tremble to begin in his knees. "Vargas killed my family. And she would've never given up on our marriage for you." Ethan felt the gun pressing against his appendix. For a moment, he thought about pulling it to make John sorry for the baseless lies he was spewing. He could shut his mouth once and for all.

Instead, he told John Waters and Mason Sharp again, "The money is right there. In one of the bags is the account and routing number for an offshore account with the last two-and-a-half million. Take the money and leave."

"Or what? You'll kill us like you did your wife and daughter? Like you killed Vargas."

Ethan shook his head, "You were with me when Vargas was killed. You know I had nothing to do with that."

"I know you left on your own. If you could pull a gun on two kids you didn't know, who's to say you didn't kill Vargas and those dealers?"

"This is insane. You accuse me of killing my own family and then Vargas. You've lost your mind!"

"She told me, Ethan!" John took a big step forward, getting almost close enough to grab Ethan. "She told me you found the letters, and she told you she was leaving."

A déjà vu sensation nearly dropped him.

"We want you to turn yourself in and answer for what you did," Mason said from behind John.

Ethan remembered the argument.

Ethan had been looking everywhere for his checkbook. The usual places all turned up nothing. He knew Kristina sometimes used the checkbook to pay bills that charged fees for online payments. She hated paying a convenience fee and, as an act of revolt, would pay with checks to make it less convenient for the company.

He went into her office, which she used as a reading room more than an office. But there was a desk with a computer in case she decided to work from home. Of course, even when she did, she usually wrapped herself in a blanket and found the spot on the couch that curved to her body.

Ethan walked to the desk, pulling at the first drawer, which was where she usually kept the bills and important documents. Strangely, the drawer had been locked. She never locked anything, not even the front door half of the time. Ethan dug around the stacks of paper on the desk for the key, frustration building as he wasted time searching for something he shouldn't have to. All he wanted was the damn checkbook, not to go on a wild goose hunt.

He finally found the key tucked behind her James Patterson section of the bookcase. Ethan huffed his way back to the desk, unlocking the top drawer, and pulling it open. He grabbed his checkbook, which rested on the top of a few folded sheets of yellow legal pad paper. As he started to close the drawer, pissed off that he had spent so much time on something so simple, his curiosity began to pull at him. Why lock the drawer at all?

He pulled the three sheets of folded papers out, opening the first one and reading it. His heart split as the words from the page processed in his mind. Someone was telling *his* wife how beautiful she was. How lucky *they* were to have her. Someone was telling her how much they cherished holding her, kissing her, and making love to her. They couldn't wait for her to be all theirs, so they would never have to share her again. Ethan scanned down the page.

With ALL my Love,
John.

John who? The only John he knew was John Waters. His best friend since college, the best man at his wedding. So, clearly, it had to be someone he didn't know.

"What are you doing in here?" His wife's shaky voice pulled him from the letters. He stood from the seat, throwing them at her, but they fluttered lifelessly to the ground.

"Who is he? Who is John."
Shame caressed her face, "I'm sorry. We didn't want you to find out like this."

"We who? Who the fuck is he?!"

Her eyes told him, but he needed to hear it.
"*John.*"

"My best friend John?"
She only nodded.

"I want you out tonight," Ethan's voice seethed. "Get your shit and get out. I can't believe you'd do this to me."

"What about me?" She asked, reaching for his arm as he tried to pass her.

"You? You're the one sneaking around on me. Don't you dare try to turn this into my fault!"

"You're never here, Ethan. I've been lonely and I ran out of excuses to tell Mary about why you're never home."

"So that gives you the right?" Kristina shook her head. "I'm not saying it was right, but I felt alone. He was there."

"Well, at least you'll have a place to go. Now get your filthy hands off me." He tugged his arm away.

"You should go," she mumbled. "Mary and I will stay here. I don't want to have to explain why we are going somewhere else. Not yet."

Ethan saw red, which frightened him enough to bring him back. "You are *not* taking her. I'm the district attorney, trust me when I say you will be lucky to ever see her again. And if you think you're getting the house, you really are out of your mind. You can stay downstairs until you find a place to go, but I want you out of our lives."

Ethan forced himself past Kristina and then headed down the hall to Mary's room.

The next afternoon, Ethan walked the two blocks from his office to John's. His blood still bubbling from the confrontation with Kristina the day before. He couldn't shake the image of Kristina and John together, their bodies pressed together in his bed. Their lips caressing the way she had promised was only for him. The crisp fall air cooled him enough during the walk he thought he could have somewhat of a conversation before he punched John. The betrayal was strong enough to nearly lock his fists in a clench.

Ethan went into the building, bypassing the front desk, and headed straight for the elevator which took him to the third floor. As if on autopilot he went to the third office on his right, barging in. He knew the door leading to the private offices would be locked, forcing him to stop by the reception desk this time. The woman behind the counter was new. She hadn't been there when he stopped by the week before to meet John for lunch, which he had supposedly forgotten and scheduled a meeting. Now, Ethan knew, he was probably with Kristina. The woman slid a Plexiglas window open, offering a friendly and slightly seductive smile. Her blond hair had long black streaks mixed throughout, matching the dark mascara painted onto her eyelashes.

"Welcome to Johnson, McKay, and Wheeler. Do you have an appointment?"

"I need to see John Waters."

The woman typed something into her computer, then turned her attention back to Ethan. "He is out to lunch. He should be back in ninety minutes."

"How long ago did he leave?"

"I think I saw him head out ten to fifteen minutes ago." She offered him another seducing smile. "May I leave a message?"

"No, that's fine." Ethan left the office. His house was only a ten-minute drive from John's office, which meant if he left now, he could catch John and Kristina red-handed. It would be all the fuel he'd need to get custody of Mary.

Ethan reached the gated entrance to his community. He looked down at his watch, noting it was almost three. The guard rarely patrolled the community, assuming with a gate and keypad, it was an unnecessary task. Martin preferred to spend his time on watch perusing the magazines homeowners donated.

Ethan extended through his window to enter his pin, stopping himself. He had an unexplainable sense pulse through him that he shouldn't use his own combination. Not that it would matter once he confronted John and his wife, but still, the sensation forced his hand away. The community, by default, made everyone's code their house number. Most people never changed them, because it required a tedious process of submitting a form to the gate, who would submit it to the HOA, and once approved, the resident could schedule a time to come to the gate and enter their new code.

Ethan entered Mr. and Mrs. Fragerty's house number. They lived three doors down, and they had told him they never changed their code because they couldn't be bothered with the process. Too many wrong entries would send a silent alarm to another patrol building off-site, something Ethan didn't want to risk.

Once the number was entered, the gate offered a low buzz. It then slid from right to left, allowing him entrance into his community. Mary would be at school, giving John and Kristina plenty of alone time. Although they would be running out of time. Kristina usually left to pick Mary up from school around then. He realized there was a strong possibility he missed his chance to catch his wife in her unfaithfulness.

As he pulled up to his street, he could see his house in the near distance. He saw John leaving, heading for his car across the street. Ethan used everything in him to ignore the screaming voice in his head to floor it, to ram right into John as he went to his car. Instead, Ethan watched as he got in and left. Ethan ducked as John drove by so he wouldn't be seen. He waited a few moments before rising back up, watching the house a while longer. After five minutes, Kristina hadn't left, which meant she would be late getting Mary.

Ethan figured she must've left before John and he had just missed her. He had just missed them together. The images of unfaithfulness Ethan had conjured up nearly non-stop since the day before intensified. He felt his throat closing as his vision seemed to blur, crimson covering the color of the world around him.

Why should she get my house and my daughter? Why should she get away with what she's done? Of all the women John used, why did he have to take Kristina?

Ethan decided; she shouldn't. If she thought she was going to take the house he worked his ass off for, then she had another thing coming. Ethan knew there was a can of old gas in the garage. They usually kept the side door to the garage unlocked, because the door to the house was always secured. At this hour, everyone was still at their offices. Those who weren't would be out for the day. Even in the cold November days, the retired neighbors filled their days with what they thought kept them young.

By the time Kristina returned with Mary, Ethan would be coming back from his day at the office. He doubted anyone would notice he was missing; he had booked his calendar out that morning saying he was in meetings. He could return to the office, show his face, and leave again to come home. Kristina would have nowhere to go, meaning he could take Mary to a hotel while Kristina would be left to fend for herself. Ethan would then start the process of filing for divorce and custody of their daughter.

As the rage continued to build, the deep red in his vision overtook him, before it all went away. The next thing he remembered clearly, he was sitting behind his desk at the office.

Chapter 39

Ethan dropped to his knees as the memories crashed into him like an unrelenting wave. The power of the wave shook his entire body, slamming into his chest with enough force to steal his breath. He didn't notice John or Mason approaching. Ethan screamed into the night until his throat burned. The memories had become vivid, so he knew they were real, yet how could he block out what he had done?

Through his sobs, he asked the air, "How could I have done that? Did I kill Vargas, too?"

John answered, even though the question had not been directed to him. At least, not intentionally. "I don't know." He sounded close, but Ethan's vision was blurred from the tears. "I came by right after it had happened. You didn't seem to know anything about Kristinia and me, so I figured you didn't know about *us*. It was convincing, Ethan. I thought Vargas did it, too."

"She didn't tell you about the fight?" Ethan forced himself up, finding John now standing only five feet from him. Mason to his side looking around nervously. "She didn't tell you I found out?"

"No. She just said she was ready to end things. She promised we'd be together sooner than we thought."

"How could it have been you? Of all the people you could've been with, why her?"

"We didn't mean for it to happen. I came by to see you, but like always, you weren't there. She was upset and started telling me about how neglectful you'd been. It just happened."

Ethan's emotions began blending, he gave up trying to contain them. They were too much, and each time he tried to hold something back, it only hurt more. "Why did you let me go a year not knowing the truth? Why didn't you call the police?"

"I didn't know until a couple of months ago. Mason was tracking down Vargas..."

Mason cut in as if John would forget a detail that would water down his perceived heroics. "I learned Vargas had fled to Mexico just hours after making bail. He wasn't in the country when the fire had been set. One of your neighbors didn't feel comfortable talking to the police, but they felt plenty comfortable talking for a thousand bucks. They *thought* they saw your car around the time of the fire, it stood out because they knew you were supposed to be at work." Mason's smile showed he was all too proud of himself for uncovering the truth. It made him feel like a real detective rather than an investigator for hire.

"I decided to check the gate code entries," Mason continued. "I found the last one used before the fire started was the Fragerty's. I went and spoke with them, and they had the most interesting story." He stopped as if waiting for

Ethan to finish the point for him. Instead, Ethan looked at him blankly, many pieces of the puzzle still missing for him. Mason clearly became agitated and continued, "They said they had been out of town that whole week. I wondered how their code could be used if they weren't home. Vargas wouldn't have known to use the house numbers, so even from Mexico, it isn't like he could tell one of his goons to set the fire. That meant it had to be someone inside the community. Your former secretary said you had left earlier in the afternoon, but you were completely calm when you got back, and had meetings scheduled, so she couldn't believe you had anything to do with killing your family."

Ethan pressed against his knees, forcing himself to stand. The world seemed to spin once he was on his feet, threatening to knock him back down. "Why go through all this trouble? What if I had remembered?"

John shook his head in frustration, "We tried to tell the police, but you had them and the DA's office fooled. No one took us seriously. We knew the only way to get the cops to believe us was if we got you to remember."

"If you'd never come back, I'd be dead right now anyway. You should've never come back."

"That wouldn't be justice. I want you to spend the rest of your life knowing what you did, stuck in an eight-foot cell. You don't deserve an easy exit. I'm glad I came out here."

Ethan grinned through the torment, pulling the revolver from its place tucked into his belt near his appendix. "I can't live with what I've done, John. I can't live knowing I hurt my little girl."

"But you can live with what you did to Kristina?"

Ethan shrugged, "I can't mourn for her anymore. Not now that I know what she did to our family." Ethan moved the gun up to the side of his head.

John screamed something Ethan didn't quite hear when Ethan saw Mason pull his pistol from his hip. The barrel aimed right at Ethan. "Drop it!" Mason screamed.

A calmness Ethan hadn't felt in decades washed over him. He was at peace with his decision, it felt right. "What, are you going to shoot me, too?"

"Drop the gun, Ethan!" John pleaded. He was watching his perfect plan unravel.

"I can't do that. You're right, I probably do deserve prison. But if I'm going to die somewhere, I'm going to die here, on my terms. Not in a brick cell, and sure as hell not by the hands of someone I put there."

"Don't make me shoot you!" Mason lowered the barrel of his gun from Ethan's torso to one of his legs. Ethan pulled the hammer of the revolver, sliding his finger into the trigger guard.

The shot that rang out echoed violently, but Ethan knew he wasn't the one who pulled the trigger. Though, the shot nearly made him. He noticed there was no pain in his body, assuming

Mason missed, he rushed to put the gun back to his head before he got a second shot. Then he noticed Mason's eyes looked shaken. The shot had confused him just as much as it had Ethan.

Mason's legs could no longer support his body as he fell forward, the gun dropping from his hands into the mud. John looked to Ethan as if he had answers, but Ethan only looked at Mason, now lying face down in the mud. John picked up the pistol Mason had dropped, facing the woods behind the house. Another shot hit John in the hip, folding his body in half as he dropped to the ground, agony belting from him.

"Ethan, help me!"

Ethan stood there, watching the scene unfold, trying to make sense of what he was seeing. John writhed on the ground, his screams turning to cries. Ethan's focus shifted to the woods but the darkness was overwhelming, covering whomever was out there. He had an idea, but he couldn't be sure. He stood there waiting for a bullet to find him in case he was wrong.

If word had gotten out Vargas had been executed and left unceremoniously in a shallow grave, someone may have come for retribution. But after standing there for a few seconds with nothing but John's screams coming, he knew who it was for sure.

Then came the third shot the thunderous roar of the bullet reverberating from the trees around him, silencing John. A few more long moments of silence passed with Ethan looking at the two dead men on his lawn. Then Beaver emerged from the woods at the back of his property, his hunting rifle aiming down toward the ground.

Chapter 40

Ethan pulled himself from the fog that had engulfed him. He saw Mason and John lying there, both dead. He saw Beaver walking toward him, a rifle in his hands. He knew Beaver had killed them both, but he couldn't understand why. He also couldn't comprehend what had brought him out of his house when Ethan had told him to stay away. Now Beaver was fully involved, but what was worse, he had guaranteed Ethan would have to answer for everything. He could've pulled the trigger and not had to worry at all.

"Are you all right?" Beaver asked as he reached Ethan.

"What the hell are you doing here?" Ethan asked, still unable to fully comprehend Beaver standing in front of him. The two men lying lifeless in the mud behind. "I told you, no matter what, stay home. Why did you come out here?"

Beaver didn't appear disappointed by Ethan's lack of appreciation. Somehow, he seemed to understand it. "I heard you screamin' somethin' awful. I wouldn't of felt right leaving my friend on his own in as much trouble as it sounded like you was in."

Ethan began pacing back and forth, hoping a thought might occur to him. "I did something terrible, Beaver. I'm not worth saving, I'm sure as hell not worth you throwing your whole life away."

"I told you from day one; I protect my land and my friends. That's why I had to put that fella in the hole. And burn down that shack. They was goin' to destroy both of us."

Ethan stopped pacing. There was a mild relief in knowing he hadn't taken any more lives, but the relief was short-lived. "Why didn't you tell me when I asked you to go looking for him?"

Beaver shrugged at the question as if it were as inconsequential as asking if he preferred water or juice. "Didn't know if he brought buddies. Could've been more out there. Also," he added with a tone of seriousness, "I didn't know if I could trust you."

"How do you know you can now?"

"We both done some evil in this world. But we done good, too." He turned, pointing his barrel to John and Mason. "These boys done evil, so did that Vargas fella. Who says they deserve peace any more than us?"

"If you knew what I did, you wouldn't think that. I killed my family. I deserve to rot in a cell for what I did." Ethan choked back the pain that threatened to suffocate him. "Listen, I have five million, I want you to take it. That way something good can come from all of this."

Beaver raised his hand at the offer, rejecting it outright. "I'm a simple man, Ethan. I don't need much. But that kind of money can change a man's life. You can start a whole new one with that. Right here, even. If you wanted."

"Even if I thought I could, I can't. People will notice them missing. I already told the police John had been missing. They'll find them, and I'll have to face everything I've done." Then, Ethan added quickly, "But I'll take the fall for them. And Vargas. I should've never gotten you involved."

Beaver put a hand on Ethan's shoulder, slowing his pacing. "There's a lot of woods out there. Between that and the animals, bodies can go missin' and never been seen again. You told the police he'd been taken if they didn't believe you, that's on them. Far as I can tell, you did your part."

"I can't just go on like nothing's happened. I spent most of my life making sure people paid for their crimes. I'm no different than them."

"That prison you've created for yourself will be justice enough."

"Is that how you get through? Tell yourself that it's enough."

Beaver nodded. "I'm not proud of a lot of things I've done in my life. I might have to answer for it all someday, but until then, I ain't goin' to hand myself over. You got a real chance to start new. Not many people get that."

Ethan looked past Beaver to John and Mason. For the first time all evening, he noticed the cold finger of the night air tickle his spine, causing his body to shudder.

He knew what he had to do.

About the author

Jack Lawrence is a retired therapist. He is the author of the bestselling and award-winning David Thorne series. His first psychological thriller, *I've Been Waiting* was also a bestseller. He lives in Indiana with his wife, their children, and their dog.

To learn more about Jack or see where his next author event will be, visit:
www.jacklawrencewriting.com

Follow Jack on Social Media

Facebook

Instagram

www.ingramcontent.com/pod-product-compliance
Lightning Source LLC
Chambersburg PA
CBHW010938140726
47988CB00010B/3503